A CANDLELIGHT ROMANCE

Come November

Virginia Myers

A CANDLELIGHT ROMANCE

Published by
Dell Publishing Co., Inc.
1 Dag Hammarskjold Plaza
New York, New York 10017

Dell ® TM 681510, Dell Publishing Co., Inc.

ISBN: 0-440-11350-4

Printed in the United States of America

First printing—October 1980

Come November

CHAPTER 1

With effort Tildy kept her expression pleasant, and regarded the man on the other side of the wide desk. If her smile was a trifle wry, she couldn't help it. She was in the odd position of being desperate to get a job she knew she would hate. Nor did she want to move inland to Sacramento, much preferring the cool San Francisco summer.

"Yes, I'm available now," she heard herself saying. She didn't like this man. There was a phoniness about him. He was what Uncle James would have called "slick"—an old-fashioned word, but apt. He was dressed in an expensive blue-denim suit and his shirt was open at the throat. He wore a thin gold neck chain and Tildy had decided that he bleached his hair. Being a natural honey blond, she could usually tell.

"Wonderful. I'll just go and set up your next interview!" He spoke with great enthusiasm.

When he was gone, Tildy's smile faded. She had to do this; she had to get this job. Uncle James was depending on it, although he didn't know about it yet. The smile returned, gentle and reflective now, as she thought of the kindly old man who had been her rock of strength when she needed him. Everybody's rock of strength. She thought of the many times her parents had gone traveling and left her in his care. He had practically raised her.

She would be honest and tell him that she didn't really

9

want the job, and she would explain why they had to have it. For once in his life he would just have to accept the idea of somebody else's doing something for him. She could almost hear him saying in his droll way, "Tildy, I'd say we got caught between a rock and a hard place." But since the job was only temporary, she felt sure she could convince him.

Another interview! What did that mean? She had already been interviewed by two people, plus the semi-professional type who had given her three hours of what seemed to be psychological tests. After all, she wasn't applying for a job as corporation president—just a temporary job in a political campaign. When the election was held in November, the job would be over—whatever it turned out to be.

Her mind turned again to Uncle James and her gray eyes clouded with worry. He had been one of those unlucky older children who had sacrificed himself for a younger one—her mother. Regardless of what his private ambition may have been in the beginning, he had plodded his life away as a postal employee bringing up his much younger sister. She had been his darling spoiled child. Then she had married Evan Marshall, who had been an only child, and just as spoiled. They had been like two children, laughing through life, never thinking ahead, always living beyond their means.

Tildy tried to shut her mind against the sudden memory of the day they died. The terrifying capsizing of the lovely little sailboat that wasn't paid for. The cold, gray choppy San Francisco Bay, overhung with leaden clouds. They never found her parents. She had been in her first year of college and, of course, Daddy had no insurance.

The man in the denim suit was coming back.

"Okay, Matilda, I've set it up for you. Just drive over to Sacramento to this address and meet this man. Marvin Logan. He's the top banana of the campaign."

Tildy took the slip of paper, wishing in mild annoyance that he would call her Miss Marshall. She didn't like to be on a first-name basis with people she hardly knew.

10

"Is Mr. Logan the—er—candidate?" she asked, looking at the slip of paper.

"Oh, no. That's Stephen Talbot."

"What's he running for?" she asked, picking up her handbag.

"U.S. Senator. Golden Boy wants to go to Washington and govern us." There was just a hint of venom in his tone, which he quickly tried to hide under a laugh. "Anyhow, he's going to get clobbered."

"You mean he's going to lose the election?"

"Has to. He isn't aligned with either major party. The idiot is running as an Independent—but with his money and connections he can afford to play games at politics." He shrugged and looked at his fingernails. "Anyhow, it's all one to us. He hired our agency to run his campaign and a job is a job. Win or lose, he pays cash."

"You mean his credit isn't good?"

"His credit is terrific," he laughed, "but campaigns are always on a cash basis. Have to be. Political fact of life."

Tildy put the slip of paper into her handbag. "I guess," she said slowly, "politics is a dirty business."

"The very dirtiest," the man said, smiling pleasantly. "Good luck with your interview."

On the Freeway drive from San Francisco to Sacramento, Tildy had time to think a bit. What in the world kind of job was she applying for? They had referred to it in several ways. Campaign aide. Special assignment. Special assistant to the candidate. It paid a salary, per diem expenses, and a bonus of five thousand dollars at the close of the campaign. None of the busy young men at the agency seemed to know exactly what it was. Apparently that information was the exclusive knowledge of this Mr. Logan and the candidate.

She was thinking desperately that if it was legitimate she must take it—if she could get it—and she almost missed the turnoff from the Freeway. Lucky she had to stay in the slow lane anyway, due to the general decrepitude of her small third-hand Volkswagon.

Then her mind went instantly back to the job, to the

11

money, and to Uncle James's recent loss of weight, his pallor. He was getting so old so quickly.

"I guess I'll have to take an early retirement, Tildy," he had said, almost apologetically. "The doctor said my lungs are wearing out before I am. Well," he had added. "I've always wanted to retire to Arizona."

He had always loved the desert, which to her, loving the green hills of northern California so much, had always seemed vast, vacant, and desolate. She supposed it had a kind of stark, spare beauty.

Uncle James would have his desert. He could retire rather miserably on a reduced early-retirement pension, or he could go into an excellent retirement community that required an initial payment of ten thousand dollars. She had often seen the bright advertising folders strewn about the flat. But even after working at every job she could secure during college, she hadn't been able to pay for everything. Without a word, Uncle James had paid the rest, sadly depleting his savings. He had never shown a shade of regret but the bright folders had disappeared from the flat.

She must get this job!

She had done some fast mental arithmetic in the agency office. It seemed too good to be true. She thought she could live almost entirely on her expense account and would have about six months' clear salary to save and put with the five-thousand-dollar bonus. That would just about do it.

She found the Talbot-for-Senator campaign headquarters without difficulty. Indeed, it would have been difficult to miss the spacious lower floor of a smart building in the middle of a downtown shopping and working area. It was even near a parking garage for convenience—an ideal location, certainly. She wondered how much rent they paid.

Red, white, and blue bunting and streamers decorated the gleaming glass windows in front and, well, that must be Mr. Talbot! Half a dozen posters with a handsome male face three feet high looked down at her. THE SENATE NEEDS TALBOT. WE NEED TALBOT. She found herself smiling. She had never been able to take political hoopla very seriously. It all seemed so false. She had become eligible to vote for the first time in this coming election, and had dutifully gone down to register because Uncle James seemed to expect it. She rather thought that however she voted it wouldn't make much difference. All the candidates were pretty much alike.

The door was propped open and she went in. She got the impression of frantic activity with an underlying excitement.

"May I help you?" She was approached by a bright-faced girl about her own age, dressed in red pants, white pullover, and a heavy blue necklace. They were certainly stressing the red-white-and-blue. Just below the girl's chin was an oversize plastic campaign button, as big as a saucer. It said: TALBOT'S FOR US. WE'RE FOR TALBOT. His picture was in the center.

"Yes, I'm Tildy Marshall. I think Mr. Logan is expecting me."

"Just a minute." The girl quickly picked up a red telephone and punched some buttons. Then she said, "Girl here. Marshall? To see you, Marv?" She paused and then smiled brilliantly at Tildy. She had a friendly, open face, and Tildy had liked her on sight. "Come with me," she said. "I'll show you."

Tildy followed her through the big room. There must be ten or twelve metal desks, most of them occupied by people talking eagerly on the telephone. There were stacks of campaign literature—folders, leaflets, stacks of mimeographed and printed material; and placards in several sizes, some already mounted on staffs for carrying, some for nailing up to walls or fences. They all bore the handsome face of Mr. Talbot. Sometimes Mr. Talbot smiled broadly, showing his extremely white and even teeth. Sometimes Mr. Talbot was serious, chin on hand, in his shirt-sleeves, obviously wrestling with some deep problem. They were lucky, she thought, in that their candidate looked like a candidate—dark shining hair, clear direct gaze, very well built, strong looking. He looked, in fact, as if a very wise committee of old political pros had carefully selected the pieces and put him together to make the perfect candidate.

13

Tildy felt laughter rising inside her. Wait until she told Uncle James!

She was still smiling when she entered the small room that Mr. Logan used. He was talking on the telephone and motioned her in, listening intently all the while and saying at intervals, "Yeh, yeh, okay, right."

"Please sit down," he said, replacing the receiver. "I received a very good report about you from the agency this morning."

"I'm very pleased to hear it," Tildy answered.

"Are you familiar with the Talbot-for-Senator campaign?"

"No, not really," she answered candidly. "I guess all I know is just that Mr. Talbot is running as an Independent."

Mr. Logan smiled suddenly. His heavy, rather homely face changed when he smiled and was quite pleasing. "Yes," he sighed, "which makes it very difficult."

"The Talbot headquarters seem busy enough," she offered.

"We're busy, all right. And this isn't the only one. We have offices set up in San Francisco, Fresno, San Luis Obispo, Los Angeles, San Diego—you name it, Talbot's there."

He picked up the single typewritten page before him.

"Your resume says you majored in Library Science at the University of California in Berkeley."

"Yes, I did. I received my degree. Eventually I'd like to work in the University Library."

"And you also did some theater work. What kind? Acting?"

"Some acting, yes. Mostly, I liked working on the sets. I helped with the one we used for *The Lark*. It was a raked stage. All grays. Stark and effective, they said." She stopped. She mustn't seem to chatter.

"But you did some acting."

"Small parts. I had to keep to the small parts because I worked a lot. The jobs came first. If the part was small, it was easier for someone else to fill in if I picked up another temporary job for a few days."

14

"And you are free now to take on a six-month assignment?"

"Yes." There was that assignment again. She was about to ask what it was when he continued.

"And it says you are free to travel." He was looking thoughtfully over her head. "It would be necessary for you to go with the campaign tour, and he's booked almost solid in speaking engagements—that is, he will be—for the next six months. Right down to the wire."

"Yes, I'm free to travel. I understand there is a travel allowance."

"Yes, of course."

"And I would travel with the candidate?" Tildy wasn't sure she could stand that too handsome face, smiling or in deep thought, for six whole months. Then she remembered the money.

"Mr. Talbot wants to talk with you himself before any decision is made—you understand?"

"Certainly. Shall I have an appointment with him?"

"He's available now. He's got two hours at home before an address he's giving this evening in Stockton. Then he'll be working in southern California for two days—I think. Let me see." He picked up black-rimmed glasses and put them on, swiveling his chair to look at the chart on the wall beside him. It said APPEARANCES. Then she noticed a hand-lettered sign in red above it that warned: DON'T SCHEDULE ANYTHING FOR MR. TALBOT WITHOUT CLEARING IT WITH MARV!!! Far down on the wall beneath the schedule was a further warning: DID YOU CLEAR IT WITH MARV??? Between these two stern admonitions was a large chart showing Mr. Talbot's list of appearances. There were not many empty spaces. A quick glance told her that Mr. Talbot seemed willing to make a speech any place any time—evenings, Sundays, and holidays not excepted. He must certainly be the hardest-working candidate in the race. She must credit him with that.

En route to Mr. Talbot's Sacramento apartment, in Mr. Logan's large air-conditioned car, Tildy suddenly remembered that she had forgotten to eat lunch and hoped Mr. Talbot would be too busy for a long interview.

"Has your health always been pretty good, Miss Marshall?" Mr. Logan asked her.

"Yes, why?"

"Well, if he accepts you, you'll find the campaign trail takes some getting used to. It's rugged."

"Mr. Talbot got used to it," she said reflectively.

"Believe it or not, it took him awhile." Mr. Logan laughed. "I'll say this for him, he's a good candidate. No matter how tired he gets, he never loses his cool."

"I guess that's important," Tildy agreed.

"Yes, it is. If a candidate gets mad or emotional, the press never lets anyone forget it. We're almost there. It's just around the corner."

"Mr. Talbot would never give way to any emotion like that?"

"Never. No way. That guy is *something*. All smooth and pleasant outside. A real charmer. Underneath—solid iron."

Tildy had to laugh. She liked Mr. Logan.

"What is your connection with him?" she asked.

"Me? I'm his hireling. I work for the promotion agency he engaged to run this campaign on the nuts-and-bolts level. From now until November I belong to Talbot."

"And in November will you vote for him?" Tildy couldn't resist asking.

Mr. Logan had stopped the car in the parking lot of a large building. "You know, it's a funny thing. If I do, it will be a first. I don't much believe in the Independent candidate. I don't think he can make it without a big party organization." He shrugged. "Odd, though. Just the other day I was wondering if I should vote for him."

"Do you listen to what he says? His speeches?"

Mr. Logan didn't answer for a moment and she glanced over at him. He was smiling.

"My dear," he said gently, "we write them."

CHAPTER 2

Although the man at the agency had implied that Stephen Talbot had money, it was not crassly apparent in his rather plain apartment. The living room was spacious but simply furnished, with a small balcony outside. They were so high up, she could not hear any traffic noise.

"Steve, this is Miss Marshall. The agency spoke to you about her."

Tildy smiled pleasantly. Then she realized, feeling a bit shaky, that this was the candidate, the man who had enough money to play at politics while other men mortgaged their life savings to participate. And that he was—she couldn't really believe it—even better looking than his three-foot-high posters.

"Please sit down, Miss Marshall. We'll talk awhile and if things work out, we'll go in and meet the rest of the staff."

In one hand he was loosely holding a sheaf of papers. His hand looked strong, well-cared for. She realized that he was physically very strong, with a kind of held-in strength, as if he had more than he bothered to use. It was apparent in the animallike grace with which he moved. He was dressed casually but she knew that the casual look had not come cheaply.

"What is that?" she asked suddenly, leaning forward. On top of the papers there appeared to be a picture of her. She was seated at a desk, her mouth slightly open, obviously talking.

"Just a photograph," he said, handing it to her.

"Of me!"

"Yes, do you want to see the others?" He held them out to her. "The agency took them during your first interview."

"But—there wasn't any camera. I mean, I didn't see any."

He smiled now, revealing perfectly splendid teeth.

"The applicant isn't supposed to see it, Miss Marshall. The camera is concealed. No point in making an applicant nervous, is there?"

"But why?"

"So we could see what you looked like," he said reasonably.

"And it was a month between interviews. I'll bet you checked up on me."

"Job applicants are usually checked on, Miss Marshall." He spoke pleasantly. "But that's too timid a term. We investigated you. Quite thoroughly." There seemed a shade of insolence in his tone.

"Investigated!" She wondered if he was baiting her, perhaps trying to see if he could upset her. She was sorry her annoyance was so visible.

Now he sat down opposite her, leaning forward.

"Don't be irritated, Miss Marshall. I'm going to be very candid with you. I studied law in graduate school and was admitted to the California Bar, as my father and grandfather had been. However, I wanted to work in politics. There is a lot to be done in this country. I've worked very hard toward this for the past ten years. My family, my friends, and I have invested a lot of money in this endeavor. A great deal depends on me now. And politics in this country is full of strange risks and hidden pitfalls. Fortunately, all I have ever done can stand the light of publicity. I am 'Mr. Clean' as they say. But I'm the outsider, Miss Marshall. I am not aligned with either political party. It's just me and my organization. But the others are out there. They would like me out of this Senate race.

18

They don't want me to split off any votes that might have come to them. Don't you see that *anybody* I take into my organization now must be investigated?"

"Yes, I—guess I understand. I shouldn't have let it surprise me. But—" Suddenly she had to smile. "How could you have investigated me? I haven't done anything. I'm nobody."

He laughed and so did Mr. Logan, who was seated on the arm of a chair. They were watching her intently.

"Oh, but you have the usual record, Miss Marshall. You were born—that started it. We live in a world of data, all of it faithfully recorded somewhere—usually in computers. You attended schools. You grew up. You have received two citations for traffic violations. You have a Social Security number. You have been employed. You participated in an inquest when your parents died—I'm very sorry about that. You have registered to vote, and I was pleased that you considered yourself an Independent." He was smiling now in a perfectly charming manner. Mr. Logan was right about the charm. "And," he continued, "you have just been given a battery of the most sophisticated personality tests so far invented."

She wasn't angry anymore. It was like some weird game, and strangely fascinating.

"And what did they show? My test results?" she asked. "Am I suited to the job—whatever it is?"

The smile reached his eyes, which were a warm brown.

"Unbelievably suited. I was stunned, Miss Marshall. You are one of the most unusually *honest* persons I have ever encountered."

"Honest? What has that to do with it? Will I be handling money in the campaign?"

He didn't reply but turned instead to Mr. Logan.

"Marv, I forgot to tell you. The rest of the committee is in the library, working on some odds and ends. Could you go help? I'll be leaving for Stockton shortly." Pleasantly, tactfully, he was getting rid of Mr. Logan. Mr. Logan knew it and got up, grinning at Tildy.

"What did I tell you? Very smooth."

The candidate got up from his chair and leaned against

19

a heavy table. After Mr. Logan had gone and had shut the door behind him, there was an odd little pause. Tildy was aware that she had this powerful man's complete attention. It made her uncomfortable.

"Taking our research at its face value, I am going to speak to you in utmost confidence. Will you give me your word that this conversation will not be repeated?" Then, seeing her uncertainty, he added, "That commits you to nothing beyond keeping a confidence."

She smiled slightly, wondering if he even realized the extent of his magnetism. Mr. Logan might say that he had charisma.

"Yes. I will hold it in confidence. I won't repeat anything."

"Thank you. I want you to look this over. Take your time." He handed her some typewritten sheets. Then she glanced up.

"Is this you? It says 'Candidate Profile.'"

"Yes."

So this was the way it was in an important political campaign. Everything down in black and white. All toted up into Candidate Assets and Liabilities so that men in smoke-filled rooms could study, evaluate, and make decisions on what to emphasize and what to gloss over or hide. She read it carefully, learning a lot about Mr. Talbot in the process. She put it down on her lap and looked up at him with her smoky gray eyes.

"Have you finished?" His voice was remote, quiet, and she had the feeling that it had been difficult for him to show her that profile. But he had done it anyway.

"Yes."

"Do you recall the first two items listed as my weaknesses?"

"I wouldn't consider the first one a weakness," she said drily. She glanced down at the profile. "Too much money," she read aloud.

"For purposes of this campaign that is considered a weakness. A vulnerable point. If I were running just in Hillsborough or down in Beverly Hills or Palm Springs, it might be an asset, but I am running statewide. That means all economic classes. Too much money says to some of the voters: 'Rich guy. Don't trust him.' "

"Can they trust you?" She was sorry the moment she said it. It sounded unkind.

"Yes, but they don't know it. I plan to be the best Senator that California ever sent to Washington. But nobody knows that for sure except me." He was looking away from her, over her head, out toward the balcony and the bright afternoon sunlight. She thought, *If he isn't telling the truth, he is the best actor I have ever seen.*

"Did you notice the other weakness?" he asked.

"No wife and children."

"Look at these." He reached over onto the table and picked up a sheaf of different-sized campaign folders.

She took them and riffed through them, glancing at happy family groups. These were the other candidates. They had wives, children, grandchildren, and dogs. All very *family*.

"Well," she said with some sympathy, "there was Governor Brown. He won and he was single."

"Brown had a powerful political party behind him. The columnists are beginning to hammer at me about it." Again he took papers from the table—photocopies of political columns from the newspapers. She scanned them quickly with increasing annoyance at their unfairness. They overstressed Stephen Talbot's marital status. Not once was he referred to as just a candidate for Senator. There was always a tag line referring to him as a "bachelor" or "only unmarried candidate" or something similar. It really was unfair. Whether the man was married or not was certainly his own business, and had nothing to do with his qualifications.

"Can't something be done about it?"

"I intend to do something. I intend to present them with a lovely fiancée. She's going to have a job in my Sacramento office. After a couple of weeks some photos will be planted in the papers, showing that we go out together. Then when they start asking, I'll let it leak that I am engaged to be married as soon as the campaign is over. Then, as my campaign aide, she will travel with me

21

on the tour. She will not be family in the sense of wife but she will be the pretty female face gazing at the candidate while he makes his speech. The impression will be right."

Tildy felt her mouth drop open in the realization of what he was actually talking about.

"You mean *me*," she gasped.

"If you would like the assignment. It pays well. It's not binding after the election." He was smiling. "In your application you said you liked to travel. I can promise you you will visit every corner of your home state. Then, after the campaign . . ." He shrugged.

"After the campaign—what?"

"After the campaign you will have traveled over the extent of California, which has about a thousand miles of coastline and extends inland over three hundred miles. It includes a lot of beautiful country. And you will have a cash bonus of five thousand dollars and a good reference for your next employer." He was smiling that winning smile again. "After the campaign you will make a graceful statement to the press—we will prepare it for you. The engagement has been terminated. You stuck by me through the campaign because you believed in what I stand for, but along the way you realized that you do not want to be a political wife—too little privacy or some such reason. You needn't worry about the statement. It will be convincing enough to satisfy the press. And it will at least shut them up for now about my being single. Consider it a moment. What do you have against it?"

"Well—it's so—phony. Such a fake."

"The honest Miss Marshall. It isn't, you know. It's just window dressing. Whether or not I am married is not important, but if it is continually stressed, it might turn off some of those who might vote for me. And maybe I can do a better job than either of the married candidates. What has my bachelorhood got to do with my ability to do the job?"

Tildy looked at him soberly. He was right about that. But to *hire* a fiancée! There seemed no reason why this handsome, healthy, and rich man should have to do that.

22

Then she realized that there was a very good reason. He must have grown up being a target for eager women. When he married, he wanted to do so in his own good time. He must know any number of girls who would leap at the chance of posing as his fiancée for a few months. His problem after the election would be to terminate the arrangement. Few girls would be able to resist the temptation to try to hold him to a real marriage. He had to have someone to whom it was just a job, an employee, someone he could control.

"And there is another matter," he was saying. "Do you know why I sent Logan out? Do you know why my Executive Committee is stashed in the library waiting? Well, it's because you and I must be the only two living people who know for sure that we do not intend to marry. The wise ones like Logan and some of the others may make a good guess at what I'm doing, but it is safer in politics to work on a need-to-know basis. Nobody will ask."

"But you said you were going to be the best Senator. How can you be the best anything, if you have to get it by lying?"

"Miss Marshall," he sighed, "have you ever heard about the recipe for rabbit stew in that early American cookbook? It begins, 'First catch the rabbit.' I can't begin to be anything in politics unless I first win the office. And I can't possibly be elected if I don't play the game by the existing rules—whether I like them or not."

She was quiet for a long time. She understood it, but she didn't like it. She didn't like this Stephen Talbot either, this lean, strong man watching her so intently. She glanced up to find his sober gaze still fixed on her. He was a man of implacable hardness, his shrewd, intelligent mind focused solely on that Senate seat in Washington. One way or another he would get it if he possibly could. How different he was from Uncle James, whose hands were beginning to shake when he lifted his coffee cup. It wasn't fair.

"You aren't going to cry, are you?" His voice sounded kind. Oh, he was clever. All she needed was a little push toward the job and she would take it. He knew that. He

23

knew she needed the money. He had so thoroughly checked into her background. Money had long been one of his weapons and he knew how to use it.

"Would anything else be expected of me?" Her voice sounded small and this embarrassed her.

"Rather a great deal, I'm afraid." Now he sounded sincerely apologetic.

"Like what?" Her gray eyes were pools of darkness.

"You will have to go through all the motions of being a campaign aide. You'll probably have to do a little of the work to make it look right. But the main thing is, I want you there when the TV cameras are on me, when the reporters are, when the public is crowding around. You will become very tired. You'll be exhausted some of the time, and that's the hard part. Because no matter how tired you are, no matter how many people you have appeared before on that day, you have to meet each new group of people as if they are the first. You will always be 'on,' with an eager, happy smile. Sometimes it takes a bit of acting. You will smile until your face hurts. I've told myself that if I ever start smiling into my shaving mirror I'll quit." He grinned a little.

She couldn't respond and he sobered instantly, looking directly into her eyes. "Miss Marshall, did you ever really watch Nancy Reagan during any Reagan campaign?"

"No, I don't think so."

"Well, of all the political wives, I think she gives the best performance. She must have heard every speech a thousand times, but the moment Reagan starts talking, those wide eyes turn to *him*. And she *gazes*. Everyone watching gets the impression that it's the first time she's heard the speech, and that she thinks it's great. Maybe she does. Maybe she loves the man. I don't know the Reagans that well. Could you do something like that?"

"Could I explain it to my uncle?"

He looked regretful. "I'm sorry, but no. No one. I'm not even planning to discuss it with my family."

"But won't they suspect anyhow? You don't know me."

"I will have known you for a couple of weeks in the Sacramento office before the story breaks. And besides," he paused, "they understand politics. They've been in the background of it for some time. If I don't give a lot of details, they won't ask."

"I see."

"Can you handle it with your uncle—without telling him? He won't be hurt, will he?" A nice human touch. He was quite a politician.

"I can handle it," she said grimly.

"You're accepting the assignment?"

"Yes." Then she added in desperation. "But you said your investigation showed that I'm honest. Why did you think I could do it—do something like this?"

"Because when you promise to do a job, you do it. As far as I can discern, Miss Marshall, you have never broken your word in your life. And there were other things——"

She wished desperately that he would stop looking at her. "What other things?"

"Loyalty, for one," He smiled faintly again. "Loyalty is a fine and lovely thing. We have too little of it. But it seems when you give your loyalty to someone, he has it for life. If you become my employee, I shall have your loyalty throughout the campaign. That is—important."

She had the impression that he had been going to say something else and had smoothly changed it.

"Are you one of my workers, Miss Marshall?"

She took a shaky breath. Of course she was one of his workers. She was five thousand dollars' worth of worker, plus salary and per diem. She was buying Uncle James's ticket to the bare and arid desert that he loved.

"Yes. And I'll try to do a real job," she said firmly.

"Good." He was brisk now. "I shall be in southern California for the next two days."

Tildy swallowed a bubble of frantic laughter. He didn't have to look at any schedule of appearances. He *knew* where he was going to be at any given time, and what he would be doing there.

"I want you to spend the next few days selecting your basic wardrobe and reading campaign material. The campaign material I want you to see is in this apartment. Always leave it here. I'll show you where. I'll give you a key. I will also give you a key to a small apartment across town that we have rented. It's yours for the duration of the campaign. You won't be in it much, but you'll want a place to rest in privacy when you get the chance. Now—" He had taken a stack of cash from the table drawer. He weighed it on his palm for a moment.

She was troubled by his mention of wardrobe. She had very few clothes and no funds with which to buy more. She felt embarrassed about her simple, inexpensive brown skirt and blazer, but her yellow blouse was almost new. He would have known she had few clothes—trust him to miss nothing. This was the same outfit she was wearing in the pictures on the table.

"Use this for your clothes. And let these pictures be your guide, please." He handed her the money and a folder which contained—oh, no!—pictures of political wives in campaign situations. Wordless, she closed the folder and continued to give him her attention. He was creating an image.

"I know that carrying cash is a risk, but you will be cautious. The important thing is, you must not let this money go through your checking account or anyone else's. And you are to return that folder to me." He was thinking of everything.

"As you purchase items, please save the sales slips. Bring them to me Sunday evening. I'll be here then. Don't lose any of them. I must have them all."

"To make sure I don't keep back any of the money?" She hated it when her voice sounded thin and frightened.

"No, Miss Marshall. I trust you. But you must realize that in politics a very innocent item can be misinterpreted and presented as something else completely."

But she had stopped listening to him. She was somewhat stunned. She had not counted the money, but it had fallen apart in her loose grasp. She thought she might have—must have—several thousand dollars in her hand.

"This isn't the bonus, is it?" she asked weakly.

"No. That isn't the bonus. That is simply expense money for some clothing you will wear." He sounded kind again

26

and she hated it. She also hated the warmth of embarrassment that she felt, causing her face to flush.

He was looking at her thoughtfully, as if he were—calculating? Yes. As a man might look at a valuable object he had just purchased. "We must work out opportunities to use that blush on the TV," he said. "Most people have color sets now."

It was like a slap in the face. Tildy was trembling with anger. She could feel her cheeks flaming. She had become one of his political assets, something useful in his campaign like the red, white, and blue bunting at the campaign headquarters. All to be thrown away when the campaign was finished.

"When you have regained your composure, we will go in and meet the members of the committee, Miss Marshall. And please put the money out of sight in your handbag." His voice was calm, almost expressionless. "And is there something I can call you besides Miss Marshall? Could you tolerate my calling you Matilda?"

"Matilda is a name I've always despised. Please call me Tildy."

"Tildy, then. I had hoped it would be something like that. It's charming. The press will like it. They prefer to nickname the political people. Ike. Mamie. Jack. Jackie. Jerry. Jimmy. That's why I'm suddenly 'Steve.' I've never been called anything but Stephen in my life. It takes some getting used to. Would you like to come with me now? I want you to meet the committee."

"Mr. Talbot." She spoke with firmness.

"Try getting used to Steve."

"Steve. I—have to tell you this. I don't intend to vote for you!" She was shaking her head.

He smiled slowly. "Your vote is your own, Tildy. But November is a long time away." Then he added, "If you change your mind, you don't have to tell me."

Following him into his library, she thought bleakly that he had had the last word. She concluded that he had never *not* had the last word. Not ever in his life. And that was too bad.

27

CHAPTER 3

Stephen Talbot's library was clearly the largest room in his apartment. She thought she might understand him better if she could get a look at some of the book titles. In addition to the walls of books, the room comfortably held a large desk, somewhat cluttered and with two telephones, a conversation grouping of heavy leather furniture, and a large conference-type table around which were seated several people.

"Come in, Tildy." He turned to the group. "Sorry to interrupt but I want you to meet Tildy Marshall. I'm getting bogged down in detail on the tour, and I need a special assistant. Tildy has agreed to take on the job."

He placed his hand lightly under her arm to guide her forward slightly. She had a feeling of apprehension. They all looked so competent, so professional, so sure of themselves. What did she know about being a special assistant to a candidate? From long habit of courtesy she smiled at them.

"Okay, we'll take the ladies first," Stephen was saying. "This is my sister, Jean. Jean Talbot Creighton. Jean is an old hand at political campaigns—she's been active in them since her college days."

"Which was some time ago," Jean said, smiling. She looked somewhat like Stephen, with the same smile. "I'm in charge of women's activities." Her tone was cordial, with just the faintest reservation. She was going to wait and see.

"Then we have Vera Briggs. Vera is from the agency that gave us Marv." Mr. Logan gave Tildy a little sign of encouragement and grinned.

It was clear that Stephen trusted them all and liked them. These were his people and he felt at ease with them. "Vera writes the speeches, publicity, and anything else important, as well as doing a lot of other things. Incidentally, each of these committee members has a staff of people outside who don't come to these sessions."

Tildy smiled at Vera Briggs and received no smile in return, just a look of interest with faintly raised eyebrows. She was a slim, statuesque woman, beautifully groomed and dressed, with prematurely white hair—or she dyed it. It was not possible to guess her age, but her skin was fair and unlined. She was stunning, but she had a look about her of such smooth, emotionless competence that Tildy was put off completely.

"That brings us to Bruce. Bruce Talbot, my brother."

Bruce, remarkably like Stephen but much younger and somewhat fairer, gave her a little salute with his hand, half stood up, and then sat down again. "Welcome to the crew," he said. He was smiling what she was beginning to recognize as the Talbot smile. Bruce worked for the youth vote.

"And you've already met Marv," Stephen continued. "You might as well learn his official function—he's in charge of direct voter contact and is based in the Sacramento office."

Tildy smiled at Mr. Logan. She felt she had a friend in him.

"Then, last, we have Leonard Bishop, head of all finance and funding. Lennie and I went to law school together. Anything at all about money for the campaign clears through Lennie."

Leonard Bishop had, it seemed to Tildy, a sharp, cold face. He seemed all beige, without the distinct coloring of the Talbots, his sandy hair blending into a faintly freckled forehead and his pale blue eyes the coldest she had ever seen. His voice was cold, too.

"How do you do, Tildy," he said. "You might even call me the legal consultant, since it's up to me to see that we don't make mistakes and run afoul of the mass of new laws now in force regarding political campaigns."

Tildy was glad when the introductions were finished. She wanted out. She had had the same feeling at times in school—when there was a mountain of studying to do that she did not feel like doing, but knew she had to do anyway. She was beginning to realize how extremely important the campaign was to these people. It behooved her to know what she was doing at all times and not cause them any difficulty. She might not believe in the candidate, but she had taken the job. She meant to do it right.

When she left, Stephen gave her the keys she was to have. His fingers brushed hers and he seemed to withdraw his hand rather quickly. He smiled briefly.

"I'll have to be careful." His tone was rueful.

"What do you mean?"

"I mean that just because I've stayed unmarried doesn't mean I'm not susceptible. You don't seem to have the faintest idea how attractive you are. You must understand that we cannot possibly have any—emotional involvement."

"*I* must understand!" Tildy felt a sudden wild anger. The conceit of this man!

"Considering that our public image will be that of an engaged couple, you must realize how vulnerable I would be if you began to believe our charade. You must understand clearly that our relationship is employer and employee. You *do* understand that."

For a moment Tildy could not speak.

"Answer me, please." His hand was suddenly beneath her chin, tilting her face upward with a quick, forceful gesture.

"I understand," she said tightly, jerking her face away. A tremor went through her. The unbelievable strength of this man! "This is just a job to me. And I want *you* to

31

understand it, too." Her voice shook slightly and she hated the idea that he might think she was afraid of him. Then she realized that she was.

"I don't believe you've thought it through yet, Tildy." His tone was polite but beneath the surface was that implacable hardness. "Well, think about it now."

"I guess I don't know what you mean," she admitted.

"Have you known many engaged couples?"

"Some."

"These are free and easy times—have those you knew displayed any of their feelings for each other in public?"

Tildy felt a slow rise of heat through her body. "You mean—you're going to make love to me?"

"I mean we have to look enough like an engaged couple to fool the press. That won't be easy. Just never take it personally. It means nothing—remember that."

Going down in the elevator, she clutched at the keys he had given her and thought, a little distractedly, how silly it was to shiver on such a warm day.

There was a telephone booth in the lobby of the building and the first thing she did was to call Uncle James in San Francisco. She advised him that she had got the job and would explain about it tomorrow. An apartment went with it and she would stay over in Sacramento tonight.

Outside in the sun-drenched city she took a taxi back to the campaign headquarters, where she had left her car. She was excited and—in an odd way—pleased, but there was a queer, quivery feeling in the pit of her stomach. She held her handbag firmly under her arm. It seemed full of money—money that she *had* to spend on new clothes. It wasn't being extravagant—she had to do it. The job demanded it. It was a good feeling.

The apartment, when she found it, was in an imposing housing complex in a very good district. There was a pleasant lobby with a desk clerk on duty, somewhat in the manner of a hotel. Seeing several people in swimsuits and some with tennis rackets, she wanted to explore, but instead she introduced herself to the manager and was shown to her own apartment.

This consisted of only two rooms. There was a squarish

sitting room, attractively furnished in light, modern furniture upholstered in yellow-brown plaid, which was picked up by the yellow draperies. Projecting from the sitting room was a small balcony overlooking a green mall. She was above the traffic noise and could see the pool and tennis courts far below. The bedroom was small but one whole wall consisted of a wardrobe, so she would have a suitable place for her new clothes.

On the other side of the sitting room was a tiny kitchen hidden behind louvered doors and decorated in brown wood and polished steel. She was not surprised to find dishes and a few pots and pans in the small cupboard. The dishes were plastic, but in a pretty design. A two-burner stove and a miniature refrigerator completed the kitchen. It was certainly not planned for the gourmet cook, but she loved it all the same.

Tildy went slowly into her sitting room and seated herself on her yellow-and-brown sofa, feeling a kind of quiet exultation. *Uncle James was taken care of.*

Dusk was falling. She would probably do most of her shopping in San Francisco, but it was fun to stay here tonight. The shopping! Quickly she snapped on the lamp nearby, picked up the folder, and began leafing through it. She began to read, thoroughly absorbed.

If Stephen Talbot had compiled this himself, he was a very astute observer of women and, she smiled somewhat ruefully, he would make a good theater director. He knew exactly what he wanted to create, and he had selected half a dozen pieces of writing and about twenty pictures to make this completely clear to anyone who read the contents of the folder.

She would follow his guidelines precisely. When Stephen Talbot next saw her, she would be the perfect—perfect what? Candidate's fiancée? The idea made her oddly uneasy. She felt somehow trapped, ensnared, and she didn't like it.

CHAPTER 4

It was unseasonably warm in San Francisco. The normally cold, gray city was brilliant with sun and teeming with people.

Tildy changed direction to avoid a demonstration in the lush greenery of Union Square. She couldn't read what the placards said, but there was a small rock band, loudly amplified, to attract a crowd. Earnest demonstrators rushed around, thrusting leaflets into people's hands. Accenting the noise was the determined *clang clang clang* of a Powell Street cable car, its conductor probably hoping fruitlessly that the automobiles would get out of the way.

Toward noon, Tildy was becoming hot and tired but delighted with her shopping expedition. There was nothing quite so pleasant as to find exactly what one wanted.

She was frequently glad today that her mother's tastes had been expensive, so she was never intimidated about going into the better shops. Even if poor Daddy hadn't ever been able to pay the bills, it had given her good practice in learning about quality clothing.

Being by nature a very selective shopper, Tildy did not have her list completed by the time Saturday afternoon drew to a close. During the next two weeks, she would have to complete the list from shops in Sacramento. Most of the better stores had branches there, so it presented no real problem.

35

In the parking garage under Union Square she sat back against the worn car seat. She had placed most of her purchases in the back of the VW, retaining the small ones in the front seat with her. She had wanted to take them rather than wait for the stores to deliver to Sacramento.

As Tildy started the motor to back out of her space, she glanced into the rearview mirror and then turned quickly around. Beyond the next row of cars, between the wide pillars supporting the roof and, far above, Union Square, she had seen a familiar face. Why, it was that bouncy, friendly girl from the campaign headquarters. What was her name? Someone had called her Dottie. On impulse, Tildy stopped the motor. It was her intent to run over and say hello, to tell Dottie that she had gotten the job. Then she stopped. From behind the pillar had emerged another familiar face—Leonard Bishop, the spare, angular chairman of the campaign finance and funding committee. Quickly Tildy sank back into her seat. Mr. Bishop intimidated her and she decided uncomfortably to wait until Monday to speak to Dottie again. She pondered a moment. What in the world were those two doing together in San Francisco? She couldn't imagine a less likely pair, young friendly Dottie and grim, meticulous Leonard Bishop. Shaking her head in puzzlement, she turned the key and started the engine again.

Going home to the flat and Uncle James, she was grateful for the fact that he never paid much attention to clothing—his or anyone else's. She felt sure that he had not bought himself a new suit for ten years at least, and she also knew that the only garment he had seemed aware of her having worn—ever—was a lavender dress she had worn in her second year of high school. For some reason, it had caught his fancy. As recently as two months ago, when the subject of clothing had arisen, Uncle James had looked up from his stamp collection at the kitchen table.

"I haven't seen you wear that pretty lavender dress for some time, Tildy. Do you still have it?" he had asked.

She had told him, probably for the fourth time, that no, she did not still have it, it having been handed on to the needy some time back. That had been her own

36

private joke, which passed entirely over Uncle James's head. When she had said "needy" she had been rubbing the patched knees of her oldest pair of jeans because she had been cleaning the kitchen floor. Needy, indeed. But she hadn't known then that she would fall into this strange and lucrative job. This brought her back sharply. Driving to the flat, she began planning what she would wear tomorrow evening when she returned to Sacramento and Mr. Talbot. She had the accumulated sales slips to give him an accounting of the clothing money so far.

On Sunday, before she went back to Sacramento, she finally spoke to Uncle James about the job, and once more had reason to cherish this dear, kind man.

"You seem to be having difficulty explaining it, my dear," he had said kindly. In his gentle wisdom he must have realized there was some reason why she had put off talking about it.

"Well, it's—politics, uh—the job itself is something I'm not at liberty—it's just—" She was floundering helplessly. She had never lied to her parents or to Uncle James in her life. "I just want you to have confidence that it— that the job—is all right. It's legitimate and—"

"I don't have to have confidence in the job, Tildy," he had said. "I have confidence in your judgment and integrity. That's all I need."

For a moment Tildy couldn't speak and had to turn away her face for fear her eyes would be misty.

Nor had it been easier to talk to him about his retirement. Although she did persuade him to write to the retirement community in Arizona for their latest price list, she did not quite succeed in getting him to also send in his application for an early retirement from the post office. That would come later, he promised her. Again she had to be grateful. If she did indeed receive all that money, he would let her help him, but he was not going to obligate her to keep the job if she didn't like it. With this she had to be content.

37

CHAPTER 5

When Tildy arrived at Stephen's apartment that evening, she felt good. She knew that she looked the best she had looked in a long while. The girl in jeans cleaning the kitchen floor in the flat had receded into the distant past. Her honey-colored hair was shining, her oval face a cameo with just a hint of color on her lips and the faintest shadow accentuating her clear gray eyes. She was dressed in a slim, sleeveless beige linen dress with a square neck and a matching jacket. Most of the things she had bought so far could be used with or without jackets, scarves, or some other accessory which changed them into something else.

Stephen Talbot answered the door himself. She jerked her head up sharply in surprise. She had been looking down, observing the delicate bone-colored sandals on her slim feet, totally pleased with their soft inner soles. Good for standing in for long periods of time, she had decided.

"What's so interesting about your shoes?" he asked, grinning faintly.

"Uh—I was just thinking how comfortable they are," she said candidly. She extended her hand holding the folder.

"Come in," he said, taking the folder. "You did your homework. Is that outfit something you bought for the campaign, or something you had?"

"I just bought it."

They were in his living room now. "Turn around, please." It was a half-command, half-invitation. Tildy turned around obediently. "It's good," he said. "I like it."

Without meaning to appear flippant, Tildy made a small curtsy and he laughed suddenly, picking up on it immediately.

"I didn't mean to sound like the reigning monarch, but I do admire women who dress well. Come on in the library. Bruce is still here. He's just going."

"Hiya," Bruce said when they entered. "I didn't know I was just going—I guess he's trying to tell me something. Anyhow we've finished." He stood up.

Tildy liked this boy, so intent on his brother's becoming a Senator.

"How was your Stockton appearance?" she asked politely when Bruce had gone.

"Fine. It went well. I fielded all the questions okay—so said the analysts afterward."

"Fielded or answered?" She could have bit her tongue as soon as she said it.

He picked up several sheaves of paper from the table and placed them on top of the folder in his hand. Then he gave her a very direct look.

"Please don't set yourself up as a monitor for my conscience, Tildy. I do what I have to do to win this election. If at times you don't like some of it, spare me your open criticism."

"I'm sorry," she said contritely. "I certainly didn't mean to sound critical."

"Okay, forget it. Let's put these away. I want to show you some other things. This way." He turned and walked out of the library, the smile completely gone from his face and eyes.

"I have a small safe in here, in which I keep stuff that should be kept out of sight." It was, Tildy learned, in his bedroom. She felt odd following him into his bedroom. This was his personal preserve. There was a touch of casual untidiness about it which seemed somehow intimate. The closet door was partly ajar. A book lay face down on the table beneath the lamp. Someone had already laid out his pajamas across the foot of the bed, which was turned down.

"Do you have a safe behind a picture?" she asked, mainly because she felt awkward and wanted to say something.

He flicked a cool glance over her. "No, that would be a little obvious. This is a specially designed safe inside that hassock in front of the easy chair. The rollers are so well balanced that it doesn't seem as heavy as it is. Come here, I'll show you how to spring up the cover."

She went down on her knees beside the hassock. He did so, too, and slid his hand under the side of it. "See here, just underneath here, a little bar. Do you feel that? No, to the left. Left, Tildy." He took her hand and guided it.

"I'm sorry," she murmured in embarrassment. She had not anticipated the sudden, quick excitement she felt when his hand covered hers.

"Okay, you have it. Here is the combination. Would you memorize it before you go tonight?"

"Yes, certainly." With her hand not quite steady she lifted the top of the hassock, which had sprung up slightly. Inside, with the lid facing upward, was a small, sturdy safe. Holding the slip of paper with the combination, Tildy tried to dial the lock open. She had to try twice before she managed it and got the safe door unlocked.

"I'm uneasy about knowing your safe combination," she said uncertainly.

"You need not be," he answered coolly. "It's changed periodically—everyone is more protected that way. Now notice that fat brown folder. That is the campaign data I've selected for you to read. I think it is information you might need. It also contains a lot of my personal thoughts on a number of state and national problems. This is all strictly confidential, you understand, because I have some very sensitive information here."

"I understand," Tildy said weakly.

He put the folder he held, and some other papers, into the safe, and shut the door, spinning the lock.

"When you come here at any time when I'm not here,

41

and want to get into that safe—or for any other reason—you have to detrip the alarm system. There is a sensor system in the floors beyond the entry hall which is wired with a silent alarm into the police department. I'll show you where the switch is near the front door. I trip it when I leave the apartment empty. My servant does, also. However, he thinks he is tripping it for the other safe."

"Other safe?"

Stephen sat back on his heels, smiling a little. "Yes, in the library we have a safe behind the picture. That's only bait. I'm hoping that any burglar won't guess that there is another one back here. That library one is where any sensible burglar would think to look for one. Inside it I keep a few nonnegotiable bonds, a bit of cash, and some unimportant jewelry. Any idiot with a jackknife can open it."

"That's very clever."

"It's a good precaution." He shrugged. "I'll show you the alarm box."

Back in his sitting room, he talked to her about her work for the next two weeks in the campaign office. He wanted her to do a little of everything, and so familiarize herself with as much as possible.

"Marv will be instructing you. I've briefed him," he said. His face seemed thoughtful, as near to worried as he would let himself be. "Mistakes happen now and then, and the thing is to keep them to a minimum. Everything I say publicly has to be accurate. A lot is riding on this campaign."

"Doesn't Vera—Miss Briggs—write your speeches?"

"Yes, but she includes in them data that is furnished to her from the researchers and survey people. She can only write them from the information given to her. How did your shopping go? Do you need any more money? Were you able to get all you think you will need?"

"I haven't finished yet—and there is plenty of money left. I thought I'd finish during these next two weeks. I can do the rest here in Sacramento around my working hours at headquarters."

He looked thoughtful a moment, holding out his hand for the sales slips she had taken from her handbag.

"You won't have too many hours. I plan to be back in Sacramento a couple of times during the next two weeks."

"And you'll need me?" she asked blankly. It had been in her mind that she was to help him out with the fiancée part on tour, and not here in Sacramento.

"Yes. The sooner we go out together the better. Some of that will have to occur during your offices hours—not often, though. I'll play it by ear. But there is little enough time as it is to establish a seeming relationship."

Tildy remembered again with discomfort that she was going to have to portray one half of an engaged couple. Hating the idea, she felt color wash into her face.

He pretended not to notice, and knowing that he did notice, made her angry.

"I have three thousand forty-nine dollars and sixty cents left," she said tightly. "That should match up with those."

He went through the sales slips, frowning slightly.

"You certainly didn't buy much."

"I bought a great deal. I'm a good shopper."

"You mustn't economize, if that's what you were doing."

She knew what he was thinking. He didn't want her to look cheap. After all, she was going to be the candidate's fiancée.

"Do you like this dress?" she said, trying not to sound as annoyed as she was.

"Don't sound so grim. I think it's lovely. Okay, I'll concede that you are a good shopper and know value. Fine. Carry on. I'll be back in a moment."

"Aren't you going to put them in the *safe* safe?" she asked, when she saw him start toward the library. Her voice was still edged.

He paused and turned around very deliberately. He walked back to her and gave her a level stare. "I am going to put them in the paper shredder," he said distinctly. "This much is out of the way. Now I have only three thousand and forty-nine dollars and sixty cents to account

43

for, right?" Then he turned and walked into the library.

"You know, I was thinking," he said, coming back. "If I might suggest, since I'll be back here Thursday evening, you might concentrate on getting something for evening. Light and cool, because of the weather."

"Where are we going?" Tildy asked, faintly exaggerating the sound of polite interest in her tone. If he might suggest, indeed. He was the boss—and made sure she never forgot it.

"We are going to a reception at the art museum—to look at the preview of a summer exhibit of early American painting and artifacts. Do you think you would like that?"

"Yes, very much. A long dress?"

"Yes, please. Perhaps you already have something?"

"No, not yet," she admitted.

"That will be a good place to start being seen together. My whole family will be there and some of the campaign people. Key people. Plus all the regular guest list for museum previews. Stay as close to me as you can."

I'll stay in your pocket, she thought, but didn't say it. After all, this was really what she was being paid for.

"Well, it's getting a bit late. I guess that winds it up for this evening."

Tildy moved forward on the couch, aware that she was about to be dismissed.

"All right. I'll pick you up at about seven on Thursday and we can go to dinner first, okay?" he said.

"Fine. Thank you." She started out the door.

"I hope you will like the exhibit. It's a special family collection."

"Is it?" she asked, interested in spite of herself. "What family?"

He paused for half an instant. "Mine. It's the Talbot Americana Collection. It's never been shown—as a collection—before. But we thought—" He was smiling in faint derision now. "It might be nice to share it for the summer in view of the campaign. Good night. See you Thursday."

Seething, Tildy pushed the bell to the elevator. He had baited her again. That bit about the campaign. Angrily, she jabbed at the bell again. If it weren't for Uncle James, he could take his phony campaign and dump it in San Francisco Bay—or anyway, in one of the rivers, since they were in Sacramento. Then for no reason at all she remembered her strange excitement when his strong hand had covered hers. She was faintly stunned. She wasn't—oh, surely not—she wasn't becoming attracted to *him*. Oh, surely *not*.

CHAPTER 6

Tildy found herself fascinated by the campaign head-
quarters operation. It was busy, frantic, and exciting.
Everybody, it seemed, was totally dedicated to seeing that
Stephen Talbot became one of the two Senators from
California.

She met more than a dozen people the first day. There
were four paid staffers in this office, including Dottie; the
rest were volunteers—college students, housewives. There
seemed a good sense of camaraderie among all of them,
due, she realized, to the management of Marvin Logan,
who seemed good at handling people and keeping everyone happy.

Of them all, her favorite was Dottie, who seemed to
remain bright-faced and enthusiastic no matter how hectic
the day became. She puzzled over the idea of Dottie and
austere Lennie Bishop as a couple, and, feeling uncomfortable about it, decided not to mention it to Dottie.

She found good-natured Marvin Logan a well of political
information, and he wisely gave her as many and as varied
experiences as possible. She wondered in passing if he had
guessed Stephen's purpose. If he had, he didn't mention it,
playing it straight all the way. She blessed him for that.
Otherwise, she would have felt awkward.

On close inspection she found that his clothing, though
neat and clean, was as threadbare as Uncle James's. From

having heard his end of one or two telephone conversations, she knew that he owed a number of bills, but he never let his own worries interfere with his good humor in the office.

Tildy gave herself a crash course in the campaign literature by taking back to her apartment the many leaflets and brochures and using them as her bedtime reading. Thinking sadly that this was about as far as she could get from library work, she reminded herself that it was only temporary and served a good purpose. She wished she could bring home some of the campaign material in Stephen's safe, but he had said to leave it there so she did.

Monday on her lunch hour and after work she shopped for the Thursday-evening dress, and finally found it—gray and pale yellow organza, so fine it fairly floated. It would probably turn cold and she would freeze in it, but she could not resist buying it, knowing that it was right.

By Thursday morning she had worked several hours at being a receptionist (No, Mr. Talbot is on a speaking tour but Mr. Logan is seeing callers) and answering visitors' questions (No, Mr. Talbot is an Independent, which means neither Republican nor Democrat) and in answering mail requests. She worked one whole afternoon with Marv, sending out press releases to the news media.

"Who writes these?" she asked.

"Vera. She's good." Marv answered.

Tildy remembered the cool, classic face under the pile of silvery white hair.

"How old do you suppose she is?"

"Who?"

"Vera."

"Who knows? In this game it's usually the young who prevail, so if you ask her, she'll have to lie."

Thoughtfully, Tildy folded releases and stuffed them into the envelopes. Perhaps that explained Vera's cool dislike of her. She had felt it keenly. Perhaps it was just that she seemed too young to suddenly be some sort of special assistant to the candidate, phony as that title was.

Thursday evening she was ready twenty minutes before Stephen arrived. She had worked rather hard and at a fast

48

pace, drowning herself in his campaign for four days. An evening out would be fun for a change.

When Stephen saw her dress, he was pleased. It showed in his eyes. She turned around without waiting to be told.

"All *right*," he said. "The rest of the women there will turn green."

She was pleased going down in the elevator. This was fun—this beautiful dress, dinner in an elegant restaurant, then an evening of viewing beautiful paintings and maybe even having a glass of champagne. And he *was* a good-looking escort. She intended to have a pleasant evening.

As soon as the elevator door slid open on the ground floor, she sensed Stephen's subtle change. Suddenly his hand was lightly at her waist. She felt the warmth against her body. It startled her and she tried to resist the surge of excitement.

"Oh, hello, Mason," Stephen was saying. "Tildy, this is Chuck Mason. Chuck, Tildy Marshall."

Mason was a lean, dark man. He swept Tildy with a swift, calculating glance. Her appearance, the elegance of her gown, were not lost on him.

He looked a question at Stephen, and Stephen obliged by explaining. "Tildy has agreed to help me in the campaign. She's handling some things in the Sacramento office now, but she will be on tour with us in a week or so. You can refer to her as a special assistant if you want to." His voice was pleasant but Tildy sensed that he was guarded.

Mason turned to look at her directly. His voice was not exactly pleasant. "And, Miss Special Assistant, what is it you do for the candidate?"

With one of those odd snap judgments that sometimes turns out to be right, Tildy distrusted this man.

"Oh, I'm just a Jill-of-all-trades," she said, smiling brightly. "Steve, aren't we going to be late? It was so nice meeting you, Mr. Mason."

"Well, you brushed him off in a hurry," Stephen said when they were in his car.

"Shouldn't I have?"

"No, Tildy. He's part of the press. The press we treat very carefully. However," he paused before starting the

49

motor of the cream-colored Jaguar, "he's a guy I especially despise, so it was a pleasure—in this instance. But don't do it again."

"I'm sorry. I hope I didn't spoil anything."

"I'll speak to Vera about it. I'm not sure what he was doing in your building anyhow. I thought he was about to enter the elevator. Maybe he's noticed your working down at headquarters and thought he could get a story."

The incident placed a damper on Tildy's high spirits. Stephen was quiet and thoughtful all the way to the restaurant, which was, of course, a very exclusive one. He was, naturally, recognized at the door. A table was reserved and waiting. Somehow this got on Tildy's nerves—she wasn't sure why.

At the table he spoke again of the reporter Mason. "I learned today that he is assigned to me exclusively now. He'll be traveling with us. It's a pool arrangement."

"What's that?" Tildy asked with a small, sinking sensation in the bottom of her stomach. She twisted the stem of her frozen daiquiri glass and noticed that Stephen wasn't enjoying his Scotch-on-the-rocks either.

"It means two things, good and bad. The fact that he will be traveling with us means that the people who know have decided that my campaign is important enough to fully cover and keep up with. It also means—the pool part of it—that this one man goes along with us and then shares his information with the rest. We'll be under his very close scrutiny. And he's a man who is certainly a professional. Everything the others get first passes through him. And, I'm sorry to say, the man dislikes me intensely."

"Why does he dislike you?"

Stephen shrugged and sipped his drink. "Who knows? But it's mutual. We seem to have an instinct about it. If this were a million years ago and he and I met, we'd both reach for our clubs without a second thought."

"It's too bad that he's the one going with us."

"Yes, I'll talk to Vera about it."

Vera again. Tildy was beginning to realize that this frosty woman was very important to Stephen's campaign. "Does Vera go with the tour?"

He looked surprised and said, "Oh, yes," as if she should have already known.

The dinner, when it arrived in the hands of two waiters hovered over by the maitre d', was superb and Tildy, knowing how expensive it must be—though there had been no prices on the menu—made an effort to eat it. She wasn't too successful. She considered briefly and then rejected the idea of asking the waiter for a doggy bag and then watched the luscious food go back to the kitchen, as neither of them ate very much.

In the Jaguar again, en route to the museum, Stephen briefed her. "I've asked my mother to have you in the receiving line. There will be several hundred people coming. You'll find out what I meant about the perpetual smiling."

The receiving line with his mother! He *was* putting her on display. With increasing qualms, she realized that she was getting so deeply in the situation that there would be little chance of getting out if she wanted to.

"Who else will be in the receiving line?"

"Jean, of course, my sister—just the family, really."

She had to ask it. "Not Vera?"

"No." Again he seemed surprised. "I'll manage to talk to Vera later, after all the guests have been through the line."

Several hundred people. Tildy was sober and thoughtful during the rest of the drive to the museum.

But it seemed more than several hundred; it seemed a thousand. The place became more and more crowded. It was an elegant museum, with the lofty ceilings of another time, and a great deal of pastel-colored marble. There was, in the modern sense, a lot of wasted space, but to Tildy this added to the elegance.

As the crowd grew larger, however, the noise level rose and it became too warm. Tildy stood next to Stephen's mother, a slim, pretty, and pleasant woman. Jean was there in pale green—a good color for her—along with her husband, Doctor Rory Creighton, a good-natured portly man. Nobody ever told Tildy what kind of doctor he was, but it seemed to have something to do with archaeology. Bruce seemed very different in formal attire, looking young and a trifle nervous himself. He had got his fairer coloring, she decided, from his mother. Stephen's father had almost black hair liberally sprinkled with gray.

Mr. Talbot sat apart in a high-backed chair, easily accessible to the guests. He talked with warmth and cordiality to those who surrounded him in a shifting group. Tildy realized in a few moments why he remained seated. There was a heavy cane to his right, and his hands were knotted with arthritis. He leaned forward from time to time and then back again, as if suffering intermittant pain.

But there was little time to think too much about it. Tildy was kept completely busy with the people coming through the line. She understood what Stephen had meant about the continuous smiling. She got into a kind of rhythm, falling into imitation of Stephen's mother. Mrs. Talbot smiled at each guest, said something pleasant, and then introduced Tildy. There was not much variation. "I'm so pleased you could come. This is Tildy Marshall, Stephen's assistant" or "Stephen's campaign aide" or "Tildy's doing some work for Stephen's campaign." While she spoke the few words to each, she held out her hand and, as the guest took it, she moved it slightly toward Tildy, thus propelling the guest along.

Tildy followed suit. It became a ritual.

"It's a pleasure to meet you" or "What a pleasure to meet you" or "I'm so glad to meet you." Then, "Yes, I'm helping out where I can" or "Yes, I'm new to the campaign" or "Yes, certainly he's going to win." Then finally, "You know Doctor Creighton, don't you?" or "I'm sure you know Doctor Creighton" or "I see you know Doctor Creighton."

One after another they came, laughing, pleasant, well dressed. Oh, surely there must be more than a thousand!

Even after the receiving was finished and she was supposed to be mingling with the guests and looking at the exhibit, she saw little of it. She was new and people were interested, wondering about her. She thanked heavens for Mrs. Talbot's expertise in such matters. She supposed that Stephen, being an eligible bachelor, had previously brought girls whom people wondered about. Mrs. Talbot stayed close to her and fended off the most persistent guests with a gentle but final deftness that told them nothing but left them vaguely satisfied.

Tildy lost several glasses of champagne after taking one sip and setting them down to speak to some strange person. She had an indistinct impression of several rooms branching off the reception room, their walls covered in gray silk or taffeta, all hung with framed pictures. There were also glass display cases. What she could see was enticing but she never got through any of the doors. *Well,* she thought philosophically, *it's a job, and I seem to be on duty.* Then she turned to the next person who approached her, smiling graciously, wondering which of the several now-familiar questions he would ask.

Several times Stephen was there and she got used to his hand lightly at her waist. It gave her a slight feeling of uneasiness—this subtle air of propriety. Her first public appearance had been standing next to his mother, with his mother presenting her. It was all very well staged. There was also the popping from time to time of flashbulbs, which, she surmised, meant people from the press.

"Will this be in the papers?" she asked Stephen, who happened to be there at the moment.

"Yes, but there is no TV coverage. Vera's very irritated. They were all notified. She wanted to avoid this coming out as a society item, wanted it covered as straight news—you know, the exhibit being a good thing for the city."

So he had made time to talk with Vera. Tildy had only seen Vera briefly, through a crowd, looking very attractive in a long black-and-white etchinglike print, which showed off her snowy hair to advantage.

After midnight the crowd began to diminish and Tildy realized that there had been a good deal of food. A long white table with a tablecloth had been set up. Tildy was hungry but, since the caterers were beginning to clear up, she was diffident about approaching the table. She smiled ruefully, wondering how much longer she would have to stay, wishing she could have some of those nice little cheese things, and grateful for her expensive, comfortable shoes.

It was after two when they finally got away. They did not talk at all for a time on the way to Tildy's apartment. A montage of thoughts and recollections played through her mind—how well Stephen's mother handled this kind of thing, the lavishness of it all, the undercurrent of excitement because of the campaign, and the constant curiosity about herself, the new girl in Stephen Talbot's life.

"You are very quiet," Stephen said, as they neared her apartment.

"I never saw any of the exhibit," Tildy said pensively, not meaning to say that.

He steered the car over to the curb and Tildy realized that he was laughing. She couldn't see his face too well in the dim car interior.

"That's a damn shame," he said, laughter still running through his voice. "It was good, basic training, however, for the campaign. It's the roughest grind in the world. Would you like to go back and look at the exhibit now? The place will be empty." He sounded almost nice.

Tildy was half-laughing. "But it will be closed."

There was a pause. "It can open again if I call the museum director. He was there, and he won't be in bed yet."

"The museum director!"

"Yes. He's an old friend. He'll simply call the security people at the museum and they will let us in and turn on the lights again. Do you want a walk-through? It's quite a good collection."

"I'd love it!" Suddenly she felt excited again. Her fatigue was gone. "But the museum belongs to the city, doesn't it? Do they run it in such a casual way?"

He paused before answering. "It isn't casual, actually. They are usually very gracious to my family."

"Because you loaned this exhibit?"

"Not exactly that either." She could hear the smile in his voice. "I hesitate to mention it because I get the feeling that the Talbot money sets your teeth on edge for some reason. But, you see, it was originally the Talbot Art Museum. We—er—gave it to the city."

Tildy had to swallow a sudden gust of laughter. Of

course! They had simply given away a museum. Doesn't everyone?

It was magic, happening just as he said it would. When they arrived at the museum, a smiling security guard unlocked the door, locking it again behind them. Another came forward with a catalog of the Americana Exhibit, just in case they didn't have one with them. Another said, "All the lights are on in the rooms, Mr. Talbot. Do you want a guide?"

"No," Stephen laughed. "I don't need a guide, thanks." Everybody laughed. It was all very pleasant.

It was also a beautiful collection. It was remarkable how much Stephen knew about it. The collection included American paintings from the very earliest pre-Revolution artists. Tildy was fascinated. There was also one whole room of early American handicrafts, hand-pieced quilts of patchwork, very simple Shaker furniture, classic silver from the early silversmiths, and delicate examples of handblown glassware.

"It would take a week to really see all this," Tildy said breathlessly.

"Yes, it's been a long time in the collecting. My Talbot grandfather started it and then my mother took it over with enthusiasm. She has also branched out now into a Native American collection—pottery, basketware, weaving and—oddly enough—weapons. Some of the American Indian weapons are really beautiful, not like the functional and more deadly weapons of today. The weapons were deadly enough, I guess, but in those times, the fighter had to do something more than pull a trigger or push a button. Anyhow, in the process Mother has become a real authority on the many diverse cultures among the American Indians. She's got a good reference library now—I don't know if you are interested in it or not." He seemed a shade embarrassed at his own enthusiasm.

"I haven't been really," Tildy admitted. "But after all, they are the first Americans. And I would love to see the books."

"Well, you can browse in her library when you are up at the house sometime."

55

How casually he had said that, she thought, gazing at a round silver bowl dating from the seventeen hundreds. Apparently he was going to make a good show of it—*when you are up at the house sometime.* Almost, but not quite, it seemed real—like a Cinderella story; like a lovely, shimmering dream of life where everything was good, pleasant, and enjoyable and where people went about doing gracious things and engaging in good works.

Then, suddenly, it was shattered. A security guard was hurrying—not quite running—across the marble floor.

"Mr. Talbot. Sir, there are some reporters at the door. We told them that the museum is closed to the public, sir, because it's after hours. But Mr. Talbot, they—"

"Oh, Lord," Stephen moaned softly. "Thank you. We'll go immediately." He turned to Tildy and took hold of her arms, saying in a kind of deadly calm. "Tildy, don't lose your cool. This is the press."

Then there was a nerve-racking, almost frightening interval in the reception hall. She tried to stay in the background and, remembering what Stephen had said, kept her face almost expressionless, despite the popping of flashbulbs. Stephen would handle it. She pretended not to hear the several questions directed specifically to her. Even in her inexperience in such matters, Tildy knew that this could be damaging to Stephen's campaign. He was handling it now as well as he could.

"Yes, the museum was closed, but Miss Marshall and I came back to look at a few things.

"Yes, Miss Marshall is with my campaign for the Senate.

"Yes, this is the Talbot Americana Collection. On exhibit for the summer.

"Yes, it will be open to the public beginning tomorrow.

"No, tonight was just the preview for the museum's regular patrons and sponsors.

"No, any extra cost for security or insurance will be paid for by the Talbot Foundation, not by the city or the museum."

Inch by slow inch he was workng his way to the door, which a security guard was ready to open. He kept his hand firmly clamped on Tildy's arm so that she was taken along beside him. He was smiling very pleasantly at them all, his voice relaxed, his manner easy. To Tildy the door seemed a hundred miles away.

When they were finally in the car, driving once more to her apartment, she hesitated to break the heavy silence, then could not contain herself.

"What was that all about? It's bad, I have sense enough to know that, but what does it mean?"

"It means," Stephen said with soft grimness, "that Vera gets her wish, that this exhibit will be covered as a news item rather than as a society item."

"Did Vera cause this?"

"Good Lord, no! She's going to be furious. My guess is that somebody in the museum called the press to tip them off that it was being opened especially for a private citizen by the name of Talbot."

"It really will be in the newspapers, then?" Tildy asked in a small voice. Now, for the first time, it seemed very real.

"You bet it will. Once again, at the risk of repeating myself, let me caution you. You're going to be upset if they handle this the way I think they will—*but don't let it show*. Always *minimize* something like this. Play it down. The less said in retaliation, the sooner the whole thing will be forgotten."

"I understand," she said. "I—I guess this is my fault."

"No," he said grudgingly. "I'm supposed to be the one with all the answers. I've been in this game long enough to know how to look ahead and foresee any risks involved. I should have taken you straight home after our appearance. I suppose it's just that I'm proud of the collection and—you were interested. I followed an impulse. That was a mistake, and I can't afford mistakes."

"But it isn't fair," she burst out in anger.

"Tildy," he said, pulling the car to a stop in front of her apartment house. "In politics as it is practiced today there is no fair or unfair. It's something you never cry foul in. *Never*. You remember what President Truman said about crying foul in politics. He said, 'If you can't stand the heat, stay out of the kitchen.' He wasn't kidding. So we just take the heat. Vera may be able to do something—not much. As my sister Jean says, just keep smiling. That's all we can do."

He turned off the engine and was quiet for a moment.

"Tildy," he said, sitting back and turning toward her, "I just saw Mason at the entrance of your building."

"That reporter?"

"Yes." His voice was faintly grim. "This might be a good time to start the rumor of our engagement. It might take his mind off the museum fiasco tonight—he's had word or he wouldn't be here."

"Wh-what do you mean?"

Then she knew what he meant. Deliberately, he took her in his arms. She shrank back, but it was no use. Relentlessly, he tilted her face up and his mouth came down on hers. She thought the long, slow kiss would never end, and she was breathless when it finally did.

"Be still," he murmured. "He's right at your door, watching."

Tildy's pulse was racing. She had never had much time for dating, and the few dates she did have had been with young students her own age. Stephen was a man, older, experienced in lovemaking. This strange pounding excitement aroused by his demanding mouth alarmed her, and she twisted against his hard body, knowing he was going to kiss her again and probably again, knowing there was no escape.

"Please," she moaned finally. "Let me *go*."

"All right. Wait a minute. He's going inside your building." For slow, molten moments he held her against his strong body and then, when he was ready to, he released her.

Tildy lay back against the seat, hoping desperately that he would not realize how deeply she had been affected. At the same time, she felt a slow anger. Even if he did know, he wouldn't care! Not him. He could have any girl he wanted. She felt a blind impulse to hit him and gripped her hands in her lap.

58

"Come on. I'll take you upstairs," he was saying, without a shred of emotion in his voice.

She got out of the car shakily, with a sudden crazy idea that Mason wasn't there at all. Stephen had made it all up, just so he could kiss her. But then she saw Mason. He was standing at the door of her building, a cynical smirk on his face, holding the door open for them.

"Did you want to see me?" Stephen asked him.

"Only if you have time, Mr. Candidate," Mason answered with pointed sarcasm. He had seen the long embrace all right!

"I always have time for the press," Stephen laughed, with only a shade of grimness. "Can you wait until I see Miss Marshall to her door?"

"I'll be glad to wait—but not indefinitely," Mason said, and Tildy felt color flooding into her face.

Upstairs, as Stephen opened the door for her, they heard her telephone ringing. Motioning to her, Stephen crossed the room and answered it. She heard his end of the conversation.

"No, Miss Marshall is about to retire. Please don't put through any calls until late tomorrow morning. About ten o'clock. Thank you." He turned to Tildy. "That will give you time to get out to work tomorrow morning without being bothered."

He replaced the receiver and looked at her steadily. "Thank you, Tildy," he said matter-of-factly. "You are a good campaigner. It's been a rough evening for you."

"I guess I'm learning," Tildy answered, surprised that her voice sounded normal despite the thudding of her heart.

"Don't be too upset tomorrow when you see the papers. You aren't going to like it. Incidentally, did you ever get anything to eat tonight?"

"No," Tildy admitted. "I didn't. I was too busy."

"Are you hungry now?"

"Very."

"Do you have something here?"

"Yes, I—" She hesitated a moment and then plunged

ahead. "I have some peanut butter and crackers. Are you hungry, too?"

"Yes, I am." His tone was rueful. "And I like peanut butter. I haven't had any in a long time. But no thanks." He lifted his hand to forestall her as she started to the kitchen. "I can't stay. You have some when I'm gone."

"Are—are you sure?" she asked uncertainly. Maybe he really hated peanut butter and was just being polite.

"Think about it a minute, Tildy." His dark eyes were glinting with sudden humor. "I happen to be a newsworthy figure now. I just told the desk clerk that you were going to retire. Mason is waiting for me. If I stop to eat and then try to tell him later that we were sitting up here eating peanut butter and crackers—will he believe me?"

Tildy couldn't help laughing. After he had gone, she sat on the couch in her slip, having put away the lovely dress, and started eating a cracker spread with peanut butter. She was full of churning excitement. She hoped that the papers wouldn't make too much of things.

Had Stephen ever had a mistress?

The idea popped suddenly into her mind.

Did he have one *now*?

Was there some woman—right *now*—in this wide, sleeping city who was wondering where Stephen was? And where *was* he? Downstairs talking to Mason? And after that, where would he be? Would he go back to his own apartment—or to *her*? Tildy sat rigidly on the edge of the sofa. She could almost see him walking into some strange, luxurious apartment, and there was a woman there—somewhere. He might say, "Lord, what a night I've had! And I'm starving to death! Honey, is there anything here to eat?" And *she,* sophisticated, beautiful, expensive—

"Oh, stop it!" Tildy spoke out loud. Angrily, she got up from the sofa and threw away the half-eaten cracker. She had no appetite at all.

CHAPTER 7

Tildy dreaded going to the office in the morning for fear that the story was already in the papers. It was. The moment she walked through the door she knew it. Half the staff was already there—more than half. Two women volunteers who normally didn't come until late afternoon were there, busying themselves. Dottie, without her bright smile, glanced up at her.

"Did you see the papers?" she asked airily. "They spelled your name wrong. They call you Tilly instead of Tildy."

"Well, it is a rather odd little name," Tildy murmured. She tried to smile but found it difficult. She had better go and see Marv. Without stopping, she headed straight for his office.

He was seated at his desk with the morning paper spread out across it. Vera was standing beside him in a crisp blue-checked suit, not a hair out of place. Marv had just hung up the telephone receiver. He looked up at her over the tops of his black-rimmed glasses.

"Hi, Tildy," he said laconically. "Come in. Shut the door."

Vera fairly hissed, "What happened?"

Marv interrupted. "I just talked to Steve, Vera. It's not as bad as it seems. He wanted to go back and look

61

over a few things in the exhibit. He was uncertain about the displays in the glassware section, he says. It turned out they were okay. It just happened that Tildy was still with him. He hadn't taken her home yet."

"And that's what I'm supposed to tell the press!"

"That's what the boss said."

"They won't print it," Vera said flatly.

"Well, you have to go through the motions of trying to clarify it."

"What *did* happen?" Vera turned her cool gaze again to Tildy.

"Just—about that," Tildy stammered. "I—I was still with him, and—uh—we went back. And we were in one of the rooms—looking at things—and then the press came."

Marv interrupted. "After all, Vera. That priceless stuff does belong to his family. He has a right to check on something if he wants to."

"Why didn't he just call the museum director about checking on the glassware? What did he think was wrong—flimsy display cases or what?"

"He did telephone the museum director," Tildy said. *This was almost lying,* she thought.

Marv interrupted again. "He just told me that, Vera. Calm down. He has also talked to the director again this morning. The museum will issue a statement as soon as the director gets to his office.

"Am I supposed to write that statement, too?" Vera snapped.

"No, of course not. Look, calm down. Steve is on top of this. He's got it under control." Marv said.

"I wouldn't say he's got it under control at all. A hundred thousand Sacramento homes have this on their doorstep. It's probably also on the wire services for other California papers to pick up." Vera picked up the paper and snapped the page over, reading the headline above a group of pictures. She read aloud, " 'CANDIDATE GIVES PRIVATE SHOWING OF CITY MUSEUM DISPLAY.' Now listen to this; it gets better!" Relentlessly, she continued:

"Stephen Talbot, bachelor candidate for the United States Senate, made a surprise visit to the City Art Museum shortly before dawn today to show a museum display to his beautiful blond companion, Tilly Marshall of San Francisco. When questioned by reporters, who had learned that the museum was open after regular hours, Mr. Talbot revealed nothing about Tilly Marshall's identity beyond the statement that she works in his political campaign. Later Ms. Marshall could not be reached for comment."

Vera stopped and folded the paper, tossing it down onto Marv's desk.

"Is that—all?" Tildy asked weakly.

"Oh, no," Vera said. "That's not all. Later editions will follow up. There will be a statement by the museum director which will be buried on the back page. But there will be statements by Steve's political opponents! *That* will all be in the front. They will be deeply concerned for the public's rights in this. It is a city museum, after all. They will be very gentlemanly, full of concern and statesmanship. They will be sorry for Steve because he is, after all, a very rich man and is accustomed to privilege. You can bet your pretty face they will damage him as much as they can without giving him grounds to sue. Not that he would sue anyhow," she finished glumly. "He's had grounds before. Nobody sues in this game."

Numbly, Tildy picked up the paper and looked at the pictures. It was like a bad dream. In one picture, she had lifted her hand for some reason and it showed, slim and carefully manicured, with a heavy costume jewelry ring that looked expensive. They looked—she had to admit it—like a couple of rich social snobs demanding and getting special favors, and being caught in the act. She put the paper down.

"They don't say that the exhibit belongs to the Talbots. They don't even mention the preview earlier—all those hundreds of people who also saw the exhibit. They don't say that the Talbots gave the museum to the city in the first place."

"Look, Tildy," Vera said not unkindly, picking up her handbag. "If you are going to be with the campaign, and, I don't think it's a good idea, you will have to get used to the idea that the media wants exciting stories that sell papers and advertising space. They are going to highlight the story with all the talent they have to *make* it exciting. If a few facts get dropped overboard in the process, well, that's just the way it is. I've got to go now. I'm going to be on the phone for the next four hours. You know where to reach me, Marv. Good-bye, Tildy."

"Good-bye," Tildy said woodenly.

When she had gone, Tildy turned uncertainly to Marv. She felt terribly guilty. "What—should I do?" she asked.

"Business as usual," he said kindly. "Before I forget it, Steve wants you to stop in at his apartment this afternoon before five. He's got to leave again this evening and wants to see you first. Meanwhile, don't talk to the press. If you get cornered, it's just no comment. And as to what you should do today, Tildy, just go out in the office and work with the others. It isn't going to be easy. You will find that some of them don't like this. Jealousy rears it's ugly head. Yesterday you were just one of the campaign workers. Today it turns out you're privately dating the boss. Some people are going to withdraw friendship they offered to you. Then again, some people you hadn't been especially friendly with will suddenly become your lifelong buddies. Don't let it get to you. Just take it easy. And, oh yes, the boss said to tell you to keep smiling, whatever that means."

Tildy smiled somewhat weakly. "Thanks, Marv." She was profoundly grateful to this kindly man for preparing her as well as he could for what she had to cope with. She stood by the door a moment, gathering up her courage. Then she opened it and went briskly into the outer office.

The morning was terrible and passed minute by slow minute. There was a distinct tension and she regretted deeply the loss of the rapport she had had with Dottie, who had now withdrawn and shut herself away from Tildy, and that was that.

On her lunch hour she came across a lingerie sale and

was able to complete her list of these necessities, all at great savings. Ordinarily this would have delighted her, but today it did not.

At four thirty she left, with a cheerful good-bye. She would just run up to Stephen's apartment for whatever instructions he had for her. Then she would go home to her own little place, shut the door and close herself in for a while, taking no calls.

In Stephen's building she didn't push the button for the elevator as she could see the indicator pointing downward. When the door slid open, she stood back a bit to let the car empty. There was only one passenger——Chuck Mason, the reporter she had met yesterday. Her recent experience with the press had made her so wary that she could feel herself freezing up.

"Well, hel-*lo!*" he said, pausing and holding the elevator door open for her. "What a nice surprise!"

"Hello, Mr. Mason," Tildy murmured, trying to be pleasant, remembering Stephen's order not to brush him off again.

"You know the candidate's really not such a bad guy?" Mason said companionably.

"I——I'm glad you like him," Tildy said uncertainly.

"Well, it's apparent you do," he was grinning, not unpleasantly this time. "I don't see why you two have to wait so long to get married, though. Why not marry him now? Right away? In between speeches maybe. Give the voters a thrill. The whole world loves a lover. It would be good copy."

"*What* are you talking about!" Tildy gasped.

"Well, I wish you both the best of luck in the world," Mason said, extending his hand.

She took it with a sense of shock that Stephen had broken the story of the engagement. It was too *soon*, and not according to his plan. Why hadn't he told her? A dozen thoughts collided in her mind. She was stunned.

"Well, don't look so surprised. You're a terrific little dish. I'd marry you myself if I'd got here first. Incidentally, why are you waiting so long?"

"Well, that's the way we planned it," she said weakly,

improvising. "Steve—Mr. Talbot—thought there simply wasn't time for a proper wedding now. Later, after the campaign—" She didn't know *what* to say. Mason was smiling easily, almost benevolently.

"Okay, babe. It's your wedding. But don't forget to send me an invitation. I want to catch the bouquet." He stepped aside, still holding the elevator door. She entered and, before it slid shut, she watched him walk away. He sauntered, rather stoop-shouldered, toward the restaurant and bar just off the apartment house lobby.

Why had Stephen told him about the engagement?

Stephen's doorbell was answered by Lennie Bishop, the finance chairman, and Tildy's heart sank. She had wanted to talk to Stephen alone. Feeling strangely apprehensive, she answered Lennie's greeting and followed him into the library. Her heart sank further. There seemed a crowd of people. Didn't politicians *ever* have any privacy?

Vera stood by the doors opening onto the balcony, her hands full of typewritten sheets of paper. Two strange men were seated at the wide table. All of the men were in their shirt-sleeves. They had all been working. Bruce waved to her from the end of the table, which was strewn with a wild array of papers.

"Tildy, I don't think you've met either Jeremy or Alan," Stephen said, coming to her. "Jeremy Newman. Alan Green. This is Tildy Marshall. Jeremy and Alan also go on the tour. They both work for Marv—direct voter contact. They make all the arrangements and oil the wheels as we go."

"How do you do," Tildy said.

"You look upset," Stephen said. "Try to put that newspaper story out of your mind. Vera has been on it all day. She's placed several clarifications. It's going to be patched up, as much as a bad story can ever be patched. So forget it."

"He means printed, but on the back page," Alan Green said, smiling. He was a fair-haired man, as fair as his co-worker Jeremy Newman was dark. These two were the real campaign aides, Tildy thought bleakly.

"What's the matter?" Stephen asked, still observing her.

"Nothing," she said. "It's just that I—was so surprised about the announcement of—our engagement. I had thought you were going to wait awhile. And then—there it was suddenly—and I had to find it out from that—what's his name?—Chuck Mason?" She stopped, feeling ill-at-ease.

"You what!"

Stark, wild tension had suddenly flashed among them like invisible lightening. Every face in the room stared at her—Stephen, stunned, losing color; the two campaign aides motionless, open-mouthed; Lennie, rigid in his chair; Bruce stiff and unbelieving; Vera, by the balcony, her face almost as white as her hair, a long slow shiver going through her. She was the first to move. Her slender hands gripped the papers, lifted them high, and flung them down onto the floor. Stephen spoke first, his voice deadly flat and toneless.

"What did Mason say?"

Tildy felt sick. "He—said we shouldn't wait so long to be married." She felt color flooding into her face. "So I knew you had—told him— *Oh, no!*" She was beginning to realize what she had done.

"I told him nothing." Stephen spoke in a measured tone. "He set a trap for you, and you walked right into it."

For a full minute Tildy stood in the well of horrified silence that engulfed them all. She wanted to die. She thought she might faint.

Then Stephen was before her, gripping her arms, his eyes blazing. "What did you say? Word for word!"

"I said—I said— Oh, let me think a minute!" She cried wildly, trying to push him away. He released her instantly, and half turned from her. Then everybody started talking at once.

Lennie sounded strangled. "Stephen, what's going *on!*"

Jeremy was waving his arms, "What engagement! What! Nobody told me! Nobody told me!"

Alan shouted frantically, "Who's engaged! Who's engaged!"

Vera, almost snarling, cried, *"All right!* I just finished *writing* the releases! I'll write them *again!*"

67

Bruce shouted over them all, "Wait a minute! Wait a minute! *Everybody!* Stephen, explain it! Wait a minute. Stephen will explain!"

Silence fell again. Everybody stared at Stephen. He was by the table, his hands pressed flat on it, leaning forward. He looked around the room. These were his people, depending on him, waiting for him. He paused a moment longer and then he spoke in that too calm way that Tildy could recognize now.

"Sit down, Tildy." For the first time she was aware that she was shaking, and she sank down onto the chair nearby, holding her shaking hands beneath the edge of the table so no one would see. Her face felt stiff.

"First, I shall apologize to you all," Stephen said smoothly. "This announcement, coming prematurely as it does, fouls up all your jobs. I'm sorry. I should have foreseen the possibility and briefed Tildy more thoroughly. I didn't. The responsibility is mine. I apologize." He paused. No one spoke.

"What I had planned," he said now, speaking carefully, "was to have Tildy work in the Sacramento office for a couple of weeks, and then come on the road with us for the rest of the campaign. At that time, with due preparation time for all of you, we were going to announce our engagement to be married at the close of the campaign." He stopped. There was not a sound in the room.

Tildy looked up at him slowly. This was the political Mr. Talbot speaking. He hadn't exactly told them—his brother, his friend, his workers—anything *not* true. What he had said, as far as it went, was precisely accurate. He hadn't said they were engaged. He had merely said they planned to announce the engagement. She gripped her hands together under the table.

The group's reaction was strange. The first one to speak was the campaign aide Jeremy Newman.

"Has anybody told Marv?" he asked weakly.

"Get on the phone to him when we've finished here," Stephen said.

Then Lennie got up from his chair. "Well, congratulations. Uh—both of you," he said uncertainly, and Tildy

68

felt an odd sympathy for him. He seemed completely confused by the announcement.

"Thank you," Stephen said courteously. "I know this will change your plans for the fund raisers. You'll be including Tildy now at the speakers' tables."

"I understand," Lennie said. "The next fund raiser is that hundred-dollar-a-plate breakfast in Southern California." He was speaking absently, his mind not on it.

Vera didn't speak at all now. She had sat down at the table and remained there, pale and terribly quiet, and Tildy thought miserably, *Oh, Lord, she's in love with Stephen. Why didn't I see it before?*

Bruce came to sit down beside Tildy, putting his arm loosely about her shoulders. His other hand he placed over hers, tight-fisted in her lap.

"Take it easy," he said kindly. "Stephen knows what he's doing. This is a surprise, sure, but the campaign is full of them. These—all these people here—are professionals. They can handle it. It's no big thing. We'll just all change our plans a little."

Tildy looked at him quite directly, at his face so much like Stephen's, but younger; at his eyes, so much like Stephen's, but lighter. Of all of the people here, he was the least upset. Why? Then she knew why. Because he didn't believe it, that was why. He had known immediately that it was phony. He knew it because he knew his brother. He knew his brother would never marry some simple little hireling without social position or money.

Stephen spoke again, more easily now. Everything was coming back under control. His control.

"Bruce has just made a very good comment. We do have to change a few plans. I think each of us had better handle that first. Jeremy, you telephone Marv. Tell him I said to make a formal announcement of it tomorrow morning in each campaign headquarters. Make a celebration of it for all the workers, depending on how each office is set up. See that the group goes out to lunch, or have it catered in. The campaign will pay the checks. If that's legal. Is it, Lennie?"

Jeremy got up quickly. "I'll just use the phone in the other room."

Lennie said, "I'll check into it, Stephen. If it isn't legal, I'll see that you get the bills. All right?"

"Yes. Alan, I don't know what this does to your room reservations on down the line. From now on please arrange a separate room and bath for Tildy. Okay?"

"Yes, sir. Uh—may I ask?"

"What?"

"About arrangements. Tildy is traveling with us? How far does this go? Is she staying close to you? I mean, on the platforms and so on. I'm thinking ahead a bit. I'll get with Jeremy on it."

"As much as possible she's to stay with me, yes. And, this is starting tomorrow, you understand. After this announcement breaking as it did, there is no point in her staying on in the Sacramento office."

"Right." Alan got up to go. Lennie left with him.

"Vera. Vera?" His tone had changed subtly.

"Yes."

"I'm sorry about those releases. This, of course, changes them all. You've done enough work on them. I will be more than glad to pay the extra cost if you want to free-lance them out to another writer." He waited a moment. "Vera?"

"Not at all," she said clearly. "I will write the releases again."

"Only if you want to." Stephen was oddly persistent.

"I will write the releases again." She got up from the chair and looked at the scattered papers on the floor.

Instantly Bruce was out of his chair and hurried to pick them up for her. *He knows*, Tildy thought. Bruce knows that she's in love with Stephen. Suddenly, Tildy felt incredibly sorry for her. She wanted to say, 'It's all a fake, Vera, forget it.' But she didn't dare. The last person in the world Vera wanted to hear from was her, and she sank down in the chair, making herself as small as possible, wishing that Vera didn't have to see her at all.

But on her way out, Vera stopped by Tildy's chair. Tildy had to look up.

70

"Best of luck, Tildy," Vera said rather blankly. "I hope you and Stephen will be very happy. Will you write me a short résumé of your background? I'll need it." She turned to Stephen and held out her hand.

"Congratulations, Steve."

Stephen took her hand. "Thank you, Vera."

He knows, Tildy thought. Stephen also knows that Vera is in love with him. Tildy now felt a moment of sheer rage. And yet he had kept Vera on! Working in his campaign! Because she was good. He was *using* her. He was selfish, cruel.

Bruce was at the other end of the table. He cleared his throat gently. "You want me to get lost now?" he asked.

The two brothers looked at each other in perfect understanding. "Yes, you get lost. I want to talk to Tildy. And while you're lost, Bruce, telephone Marv. Tell him to give Vera all the background information on Tildy. She'll know what to use. And Bruce?"

"Yes?"

"Tell him to give Vera all the help she needs."

"Right."

"And then go home and talk to Mother and Father. *Explain.* I'll need some backup from the home scene."

"Right." Bruce came to Tildy, leaned down quickly, and kissed the top of her head. Then he darted out the door.

Tildy was down in her chair as far as she could get. They were alone now. Now is when she would have to talk to him, face his anger. The silence stretched out too long. She was forced to look up at him. He was regarding her intently. His face was expressionless, except for the dark held-in rage in his eyes.

CHAPTER 8

Bending his powerful body, he reached out and grasped her arms with his strong hands and dragged her up out of the chair. The grip of his hands made her gasp with pain and he shook her, roughly, again and again, making her head swim.

"Why!" he grated. "Why! Why did you do it? You just couldn't wait to trap me into a public engagement, could you!"

"No! No!" she cried. "It was a mistake. I didn't mean it. He tricked me." She twisted and turned frantically in his grasp, struggling to get free of the punishing hands, the black rage in his eyes. "Please!" Then, rescued from her panic by her own anger at what he was doing, she beat in fury against his chest.

"Stop it! Let me go! I did not trap you! I wouldn't have you! You stinking beast—stop it!"

He let her go suddenly so that she fell back against the table. Instinctively, he reached out to steady her and she shrank from his touch. She had never been so furious in her life, and the intensity of her anger made her feel physically sick for a moment.

"Marv was wrong," she cried furiously. "Marv said you never lost your temper. Ha! What's this! What's this display! Like a two-year-old child who can't have his way. And as for trapping you—for your information, that was an honest mistake on my part. He let me think you had told him about the engagement. I did the best I could! I was wrong! I'm sorry. If you want my resignation—you can have it!"

"I don't want your resignation," he said roughly.

"And about those clothes I bought," she went on, not listening to him. "About those. I can pay you back—a little at a time. But I'll pay you every stupid cent! And I'll give you back the rest of the money. Right now! I've got it in the secret place in my purse. I'll throw it in your face!"

"Wait! *Wait—a—minute!* Talk about temper." He reached out again and took hold of her, gently this time. "You're shaking. Tildy. Tildy, listen to me. Calm down. All right, dammit. I apologize. There. I apologize for the crack about entrapment. I guess you didn't do it on purpose."

"You *guess* I didn't!"

"All right. You didn't. Are you satisfied? Just the same, the damage is done. That creep, Mason, has it on the wire services now. True, I haven't confirmed it, but you have said enough to make it tough for me—tough and expensive—if you were that kind of person," he finished in a more reasonable tone.

"Yes, you should know what kind of person I am. You practically had me psychoanalyzed before you hired me. And anyhow, this was your plan, wasn't it? We were supposed to be this loving engaged couple—so that the candidate can have a feminine face gazing while he makes his speech. Wasn't that the whole idea?"

"Yes, Tildy, that was the whole idea. But don't forget I was allowing a couple of weeks before *I* made the announcement."

"Of course!" Suddenly she understood. "That was to give yourself time to look me over, observe me. If I wasn't good enough, you could still discharge me and drop the whole idea. Right?"

"Yes," he said insolently. "As a personable thirty-four-year-old bachelor with half the money in the world and a

74

good political future—yes, I have to be careful. And I've had plenty of practice avoiding entrapment."

"Oh! Of all the insufferable— Really!"

"All right. That sounds conceited. But grant me this. You can't judge me by your standards. You don't have my problems, my experiences, or my responsibilities. Don't judge a man until you've walked awhile in his shoes."

"Oh, no! Not little nuggets of wisdom. This is too much. I'm leaving!"

"No way. Forget about leaving. As of the moment you talked to Chuck Mason and got yourself locked into my life for the next six months, you became a political person. Political people can't do what they want to do, when they want to do it. Political people have to think first and weigh all the possibilities. You're not leaving this apartment until you are completely composed." He paused. "Marv said I never lost my temper, did he?"

Momentarily distracted, she answered, "He said you never lost your cool. I guess that means about the same thing almost."

He was looking at her through half-closed eyes. "That's interesting," he murmured.

"Wh-what's interesting?" She was calmer now. The rage had receded.

"Marv is almost right, you know. All my life I have been trained and schooled to retain an outward composure, no matter what was happening inside me. It's not easy, but it can be done, especially when there is always the threat hanging over your head that everything you do or say at any given moment can turn up in tomorrow's paper. It makes people cautious."

She regarded him silently. There was a film of moisture on his forehead and the steady beating of a pulse in his right temple. He wasn't as calm as he pretended.

"Does it interest you to know that you are the only person I've ever blown up at since I reached adulthood?"

"Should it interest me?"

He shook his head. "I don't know. You seem to have a strange effect on me." He reached out to her.

75

She thought in deep astonishment, *He's going to kiss me.* Without any reporters. Without any cameras to take a picture. Fascinated, unable to resist, she went limp as his arms encircled her. Her face tilted upward. Her lips parted and his mouth came down on hers. When he finally released her, she gave a sobbing little breath and pressed her face against his shoulder.

"You're sweet," he said remotely. "You're very sweet, Tildy." Then he pushed her away against the table. "And you know this is a dangerous game for us. Like it or not, there is a strong physical attraction between us. I said once before, and I'd better say it again, we'll have to be careful. I'm sorry I slipped just now. From now on we play it by the rules—okay?"

She nodded wordlessly because for the moment she simply could not speak.

"I—want to call my Uncle James," she said finally.

"What for?"

She looked up at him blankly. How could she explain? She just wanted to talk to Uncle James, sweet, kindly, nice—yes, that was it, nice. She wanted to talk to somebody nice with nothing to gain by talking to her.

"Were you thinking, perhaps, of confiding in Uncle James?" There was more than a shade of sarcasm in his tone.

"I don't know."

"Well, put that idea out of your head, Tildy. I'm sorry you made the mistake with Chuck Mason. But, actually, it was partly my fault. I should have foreseen that you didn't have any experience in fending off nuisances. I should have warned you better, explained more. Let's go into the living room. It's more comfortable. I think I'd like a drink. Do you want one?"

"N-no, thank you."

"As you wish."

Tildy sat gingerly on the edge of a chair in the living room while he made himself a drink. She felt hot and breathless. She heard the ice clinking in the glass when he came back into the room. She was regaining her composure. It was a hot day and she was slightly uncomfortable.

76

She wished she had asked for something cold, but didn't have the courage to now. She sat silent while he morosely sipped his drink. He was by that heavy table again, leaning against it, facing her. Why didn't he sit down? Why didn't he say something? Her lips were still tingling.

Finally she could stand the silence no longer. "I guess if it were a million years ago you would pick up your club and go after Chuck Mason."

"Probably." He took a sip of his drink and set it down on the table. "After I had beaten the living hell out of you first. I don't think men quibbled about beating women a million years ago."

"I'd have fought back, even a million years ago," Tildy said doggedly. He had no business talking like that. Well, yes, he did have, but it made her angry anyway.

He started to pace around the room—prowl, was more like it, like a restless animal in a cage.

"Were you going to question me about the conversation with Mr. Mason?" She had a perverse need to get and hold his attention.

"Never mind. I can guess how it happened. I'm thinking."

And that meant "Shut up, Tildy," she thought, and lapsed into silence again.

Finally he sat down in the big lounge chair, forgetting his drink on the table. He leaned back. She had an odd feeling that he was tired. She was feeling calmer now.

"I guess the wheels are in motion without any trouble. The phone hasn't rung," he said. He didn't sound angry now. Apparently he was finished with his thinking, too.

"Could you be ready to go tonight on a nine o'clock flight?" he asked suddenly.

"Go where?" Her tone held her surprise.

"With me. I'm scheduled for an early morning speech at a big church breakfast in Los Angeles tomorrow morning at eight. But I need to talk to some of the Los Angeles campaign people beforehand—so I'm leaving tonight for that."

Then she remembered that during the terrible scene in the library he had mentioned that she would not stay in the Sacramento office.

77

"Of course." She was suddenly afraid of all this and hoped it did not show in her voice. She was not ready, either. She still had shopping to do. Well, she would have to manage with what she had. She looked over at him. He was leaning forward now, arms on his knees, looking into his drink. She realized there was no way that she would have the courage to tell this strong, brooding man that she needed a few more shopping days.

Now the telephone did ring. There was an extension on the big table. He got up to answer it.

"Thanks, Marv . . . Yes, a little too sudden, but Chuck Mason got to Tildy . . . Well, these things happen . . . Yes, I'm taking her to L.A. with me . . . No, my mother will arrange something like that when we get back . . . I'll keep you advised as we go . . . It will give Vera something more to write about . . . Oh? When does he get in? . . . Yes, I'll talk to him again, but have Lennie there. And tell Alan to have the plane for ten o'clock instead of nine and I'll talk to Hallett first . . . Thanks, again, Marv." He hung up the receiver, picked up his drink, and started his prowling again.

How sure he is of everybody, Tildy thought. Jeremy would do that. Vera will do this. Alan will do something else. Lennie had to be somewhere. His mother will arrange something. And he didn't even have to tell her what. He had sent Bruce to do that. Suddenly, she didn't want to stay here anymore. She stood up.

"Where are you going?"

"I'll have to pack some things."

"Would you like to have some dinner first? We can have an early dinner here. There is a restaurant downstairs. I didn't have lunch."

Downstairs in the dining room he ordered dinner for them. They talked little during the meal, but when they were having their coffee he seemed more relaxed.

"I think I should mention something," he said. He was almost, not quite, smiling.

"What?"

"Well, I've been guilty in the past of not giving you fair warning when something was about to happen."

78

"Is something going to happen now?" Tildy couldn't keep the apprehension out of her voice, though her tone was low.

"Don't look at me with that wide-eyed fright. Yes, something probably will happen. Chuck Mason is here in the dining room."

"Oh, no. Not again."

"Don't get upset. In a few minutes he will undoubtedly come over here. Now you recall we are an officially engaged couple, as officially as his paper and three wire services can make it. And you are about to leave to do your packing, right? It follows then that I'm going to kiss you good-bye. If I don't, it will look strange to Mason. He saw us in the car last night, don't forget."

Tildy went numb for a moment. "I—won't."

"And another thing."

"What?" She could already feel the warmth rising in her body. She forced herself not to look at his mouth.

"You are new at coping with the press. After that business last night, and this trick of Mason's today, you've had your fill of them. Despite that—you must remember to keep your cool. Remember what I said about never retaliating. He may bait you. If he does, just laugh it off."

"I think I've learned that," Tildy said.

"I just didn't want you to start bouncing dishes off his head. You have a few minutes yet. I see he just ordered some more coffee. What's the matter?"

"I just thought of something," she said unhappily. "My Uncle James. I—certainly don't want him to read about this engagement in the papers."

"Tildy, there is no way he can avoid learning about it if he takes a daily paper or watches TV."

"I mean I want him to hear it from *me*."

"Then you had better call him when you get back to your apartment. But be careful what you say," he added.

"I mean—I would like to go and see him and tell him."

"That isn't possible at the moment. You'll have to handle it by phone."

Just like that. It was an order, no mistake about it. She could feel the color rising into her face. If she were the

79

type to throw dishes, it wouldn't be at Chuck Mason, but at Stephen Talbot.

"Maybe in the next week or so, when we have a break, you could go and see him. Or, if you think it's vital that someone see him to explain, I'll send Jean over."

"Jean? Your sister? What good would that do?"

"She has more free time than you have at the moment. If you think a personal face-to-face talk would ease his mind, she could handle it for you. She's a born diplomat. She's also a very nice person."

Tildy clasped her hands in her lap and mentally counted to ten. Then she made it twenty. Everything had to go *his* way.

"What happens to a person's private life in politics?" she asked after a moment.

When he replied, his voice was quite hard. "I, and temporarily, you, are public figures. Public figures belong to the public. It's that simple. Private life is enjoyed— when you have time—around the edges. The public commitment comes first. You'll have to remember that. Right now you are worried about your uncle, a man you obviously love very dearly. I'm sorry you are worried about him. But tonight at ten we have to take a plane to Los Angeles, because tomorrow morning you have to be seated at a strange breakfast table in a strange city listening to me make a political speech there. I'm sorry, but that's the way it is. It—takes some getting used to, I'll concede that. Do you want to have Jean go over to San Francisco tomorrow?"

"No," she said. "I'll telephone from my apartment. And I'll be careful what I say," she added, an edge to her voice.

"Please do. And be careful now. Chuck Mason is coming this way. And I hate to mention it, but you're looking a bit grim. Can you smile?"

She made herself smile at him when Chuck Mason arrived.

"Hi, is it okay if I speak to you a minute—or aren't you speaking to me?"

He had stopped at their table, and Stephen was getting

up, holding out his hand in the friendliest possible manner. "Would you like some coffee? Liqueur?"

"No, thanks. I've just finished." Both men were looking at Tildy.

She would show them. She had had, after all, some drama training. She could be as phony as they were. She flashed him her most brilliant smile.

"Mr. Mason, how nice to see you."

"No hard feelings?" His voice was tentative.

"No. I don't think Stephen was too happy about the early disclosure of the engagement but——" She shrugged. "Now he can't get out of it. He can't change his mind when it's already on the wire services, can he?"

"I don't think I'd change my mind," Stephen said, sounding warm and relaxed, which she knew he was not.

"You've got quite a girl there, Talbot. You know it?"

"Of course I know it," Stephen said easily. "She's the one I want for all my life."

"My paper will want to do some follow-up—women's angle. When can someone interview you?" He was speaking directly to Tildy.

Stephen cut in smoothly. "Have her clear it with Marv, Chuck. Also, Vera will have some material about Tildy tomorrow that your paper might want to use."

Clear it with Marv, Tildy thought wildly. Oh, no. Would they now put up another big chart? For the candidate's fiancée? Don't schedule anything for Miss Marshall without clearing it with Marv. Good grief!

Stephen was glancing at his wristwatch. "Tildy, you have to pack and so do I. Will you be going with us to Los Angeles, Chuck?"

"Yeah, beginning now, my boss said. I think you are a rising political light. He wants me to start with that speech you've got at the crack of dawn tomorrow."

"I'm glad to hear it. We'll try to make you comfortable."

"I wasn't worried," Mason said, with an undertone of antagonism in his voice. "I've seen that private plane you travel in. Be neat going first class for a change. Is that your own plane, Talbot?"

"No, just leased." Stephen said blandly. It was interesting to watch him. He wasn't allowing himself to become annoyed. Or, if he was, he wasn't allowing it to show.

Tildy got up and picked up her handbag.

"I'll stop by for you in time for the plane, Tildy," Stephen said, moving toward her. They were both standing beside the table. Mason had moved back. Then she remembered—but too late, so that she was startled—when Stephen took hold of her arms and pulled her to him, startled when his mouth came down on hers. A wild surge of excitement rushed through her. Brief as the kiss was, she gasped faintly when he released her.

"See you in a little while," he was saying, and Chuck Mason, who was smiling his sardonic smile, gave her a little wave.

All the way back to the apartment, she was seized with fits of trembling. She couldn't go through with it. She couldn't! She had never before—never—had this kind of reaction to any man. And such an awful, rock-hard, utterly selfish, utterly cruel man at that! Distracted, she drove through a red light and didn't notice it.

CHAPTER 9

The Alice-in-Wonderland quality had returned. Tildy looked around the large and attractively appointed meeting hall. There was a large U-shaped table, at the head of which she sat alongside of Stephen and a row of the church's dignitaries. She had lost count but there seemed to be well over two hundred people here.

There had been the night flight in the spacious private jet; the unbelievable confusion of the Los Angeles freeways and congested traffic; then the wait at one of the Los Angeles headquarters offices, where she made polite conversation with workers who had stayed late to see the candidate and get a glimpse of the candidate's fiancée. Stephen had been closeted with his key people there discussing tactics. Vera sat in on the discussion.

Now Tildy brought herself back with a start because Stephen had started speaking and she was supposed to watch him—gaze, he had said. Well, she had better start gazing. She actually hadn't heard him speak so it should be interesting, for the first time anyhow.

"I don't know," he was saying, "if it was important enough to be carried in the Los Angeles papers, but I became engaged yesterday. And before I commence the remarks you kind people invited me here to make, I would like to introduce to you my wife-to-be, Tildy Marshall. Stand up, Tildy, so everyone can see you." He was half-laughing. It was a good performance of a man pleased with his fiancée and slightly embarrassed at the same time.

Obediently, she stood up and felt Stephen's arm go around her waist. He was holding her rather close to his side as he went on. She felt his strength, his muscular hardness. He had a naturally strong and healthy body, which he kept in superb condition.

There was a ripple of enthusiastic applause. Down at the end of the table, Vera was smiling brightly and clapping along with the rest. So were Alan and Jeremy, the campaign aides. Tildy wondered ruefully how many times they would go through this charade. They were all good showmen.

"Once we had made up our minds," Stephen was saying in a conversational tone, "I wanted to marry right away, but Tildy held out for the traditional big wedding with all the trimmings. So I wait." Now there was appreciative applause along with a sympathetic ripple of laughter from the audience. He had won them. It was a good beginning for a political speech. They liked him. They would listen open-mindedly to what he had to say. He dropped a light kiss on her cheek and she sat down, feeling color come into her face. *Blush on demand,* she thought bitterly.

As they were leaving, outside in the brazen southern California sunshine, Jeremy Newman spoke to her, his black eyes sparking.

"Tildy, you wowed them. They were in his pocket from the second of that introduction. This sudden engagement was a jolt to us—making us change our plans— but the boss knew what he was doing."

"Doesn't he always?" Tildy murmured.

"I guess you're right." Her sarcasm was lost an Jeremy.

"Sometimes," Jeremy continued, "he's had hard going. Mainly I think because he's so rich and self-sufficient. It turns people off sometimes. Now, with the announcement of the engagement, he's just one of the guys. You know—has a girl, falls in love, gets engaged—just like anybody else."

"Just like anybody else," Tildy agreed. "I'm glad you're pleased, Jeremy."

There was a large hired car which held them all comfortably—she, Vera, and Stephen in back, Jeremy and Alan in front with the driver. When they were en route again through the congested Los Angeles traffic, under an overcast of heavy smog, Vera spoke. There was the feeling that she had been waiting to say this, an undertone of suppressed excitement.

"Stephen, I was on the phone in the vestry office and I think I just made a date for you to be on TV's *Face the People* program tomorrow. As soon as I can I'll call Marv."

Tildy felt the sudden total stillness in Stephen's body next to her.

"Are you sure?"

"If Marv hasn't booked you for tomorrow afternoon at two thirty, we're in."

The program *Face the People* was familiar to Tildy. Uucle James watched it faithfully each Sunday afternoon and sometimes she did, too. It was one of those TV programs with a permanent panel of reporters who questioned political guests. The newscasters were usually in the adversary position and Tildy had often felt quite sorry for the guest. But it was a political plum for the politician who could handle it, because it meant free nationwide exposure for himself and his views.

"We have another speakng date this afternoon in Anaheim."

"I know. I'm sure there is time. I had Alan change our flight plan to give us another forty-five minutes."

Stephen was thoughtful.

"Steve," Vera said. "It's such a good chance. You know—politicians will do anything to get on that show. Can you do it?"

"Of course I can do it," he answered almost absently. "What I don't understand is why I was invited in the first place. My candidacy isn't that important yet. They must have had somebody else scheduled. Notice is too short."

"They did. Senator McGovern. For some reason he can't appear. They had to rush around at the last minute for a new guest. Apparently somebody thought it might be good to have an Independent candidate on for a change."

"Well, it's too good a chance to pass up," Stephen agreed.

Tildy felt a bit sick. She had watched this show and knew how those experienced newscasters worked. She knew quite positively that she did not want Stephen Talbot on their show, at their mercy. Then she suppressed a giggle at the idea of feeling protective of Stephen. He had more than demonstrated his ability to take care of himself.

Tildy listened carefully to the afternoon speech also, in which there were subtle changes, an emphasis on different issues. This was a totally male group, an association or service lodge, Tildy was not sure which. The group applauded enthusiastically, and Tildy had to admire Vera, who wrote the speeches. With Stephen's basic philosophy to go on, she knew enough about the various types of audiences to stress things they wanted to hear and—possibly—omit entirely issues they didn't want to hear.

As they left the large private dining hall of the expensive restaurant where the meeting had taken place, Tildy felt suddenly tired and wondered about it, for it was only midafternoon.

"Are we going to stop at the headquarters here?" Alan asked.

"Whenever there is time, we'll always stop at the local headquarters," Stephen said. "If they are willing to work in the campaign, they deserve that courtesy."

Tildy felt a sense of dread. Another campaign headquarters. Another group of enthusiastic campaign workers, all intent on her every word and look, because she was the candidate's fiancée. It was nerve-racking. She wondered how the real political women did it, year after year, all through their husband's careers. She was beginning to have a healthy admiration for them, these

86

wives, daughters, and mothers of the candidates. They were always performing, always on.

"There seems to be a lot of young people," Tildy commented in the car en route to the airport.

"That's Bruce's work," Stephen answered. "He's been up and down the state a dozen times, recruiting on the campuses and before church groups and young business groups."

She leaned back in her seat. Anaheim was unbearably hot. "Where are we going now?" she asked. She longed to get back to the air-conditioned hotel in Los Angeles. She could shut herself in, draw the blinds, lie down.

"San Bernardino tonight," Stephen replied absently. "But we'll have a brief stop at the hotel to freshen up before we leave."

"What happens in San Bernardino?" Tildy asked, realizing as she did so that she shouldn't have. Her question sounded stupid.

Vera's laugh was somewhat sharp. "He has to make a speech tonight, Tildy. This is a political campaign, remember?"

Tildy laughed, although somewhat wearily. "It's hard to forget. When does it end?"

Stephen answered her, sounding hard again. "It doesn't stop until the day before the election in November." She knew he meant it. No matter which way things went for him, she knew he would keep on until the last possible moment. It was somewhat frightening. In a sudden sense of despondency she thought, He can't win, not with both cumbersome political parties lumbering along. They had most of the registered voters, all the millions of dollars. They controlled all the city political machines, had all the solidly entrenched office holders. All of them were obligated to be against him because he was outside the two-party system, because he was an Independent. All those little people, those countless volunteer workers, all his believers—he would take them all down with him when he lost, as he must in the end. She felt a stinging of tears beneath her eyelids. Maybe when they got to the

87

hotel she would telephone Uncle James. It would be nice to talk to him for a few minutes.

But when she got to the hotel there wasn't time. She was hot and sticky, so she took a shower and redid her hair, making herself as attractive as she could for the evening's performance.

The dinner speech was like the luncheon speech, which was like the breakfast speech, only all slightly different. There were also the social amenities. How do you do. It is such a pleasure to be here. Oh, thank you. We certainly appreciate your support. Thank you. Thank you very much. It is such a pleasure to be here. And on and on and on.

Back in the hotel room, she stood exhausted just inside her door and kicked off her shoes, one after the other, watching them sail across the room. She would pick them up tomorrow morning, when she felt like it. Right now she was going to call Uncle James. She was counting on the fact that he frequently stayed up to watch the late late show on TV.

"Tildy, dear, how nice to hear from you. How are things going?"

How indeed? She began to pick out some of the day's incidents to tell him, stories that would amuse him or please him. No need to tell him of her own uncertainties, of this strange depression, or the fatigue that made her hand shake when she held the telephone receiver.

"And, oh yes," she said suddenly, "please don't forget to watch *Face the People* tomorrow because Stephen is going to be the guest on it."

"Are you sure, Tildy? I thought they were having Senator McGovern."

"That was changed," Tildy explained. "Stephen was invited to fill in at the last minute. It's quite a good chance for him."

"I do hope the boy can hold his own," Uncle James said after a moment, rather sympathetically.

"I think he can," Tildy answered, hoping she didn't sound grim. She had watched him holding his own all day long.

88

"I had a nice surprise today, Tildy," Uncle James was continuing. "Speaking of the Talbot family, Mrs. Creighton came to call on me. Clear from Sacramento. Wasn't that nice?"

Mrs. Creighton? Jean. Stephen's sister.

"Uh—yes, that was very nice, Uncle James. Why in the world did she?"

"I don't know, dear. Just friendly, I guess. She's quite a charming woman, don't you think?"

"Quite charming," Tildy agreed woodenly.

"You know, dear, I don't know if you realize it or not but it has been unseasonably warm here in San Francisco. And we had some vanilla ice cream, Mrs. Creighton and I." He sounded rather pleased with himself.

"Oh, Uncle James, you did remember to use the good dishes, didn't you? Mother's dishes? The ones in that dining room sideboard?"

"Oh, dear me, Tildy. I'm afraid I used the white kitchen dishes. We were in the kitchen at the time, you see."

Good grief. The old white kitchen crockery, all chipped and cracked. And that kitchen, with it's worn, torn linoleum on the floor.

"Do you know something, Tildy? Mrs. Creighton had the nicest idea. She asked if I had ever tried nutmeg on top of vanilla ice cream. I had not, and we had it that way. It's really delicious. I suggest you try it."

"Of course," Tildy murmured weakly. "I'll be sure and try it. What else did you talk about, Uncle James?"

"A great deal, rather. The time just flew by. You know, she and all the rest of the Talbots, I guess, are quite interested in the American Indians and she knew of my interest in the American desert—I suppose you mentioned it to her. We talked about the Apache and the Pima in Arizona. She had brought me a small fossil, quite delicate and lovely, from the time when the desert was under the sea. I have it on the mantel in the living room. I'll show it to you when you come home."

"Fine," Tildy said, feeling grim. No, she had not told the Talbots of his interest in the desert. That, she supposed, had come out in the massive Talbot investigation of her background. It was so thorough, so invincible, even to the seemingly casual visit by Jean Talbot Creighton to Uncle James. She wondered what had really been said. Somehow or other, she was sure, Jean Talbot Creighton had got it through to Uncle James in that smooth Talbot way, that the engagement was just make-believe, a necessary bit of political window dressing, but also in some way perfectly all right.

And somehow or other, with all the other matters on his mind, Stephen had decided to send Jean over to San Francisco on this errand—even after she had told him not to. Everything had to go his way. He never missed anything, never overlooked anything. When they rang off, she replaced the receiver, her eyes stormy. She was angry, a little apprehensive and suddenly fiercely protective about Uncle James.

CHAPTER 10

Tildy had no time in the morning to worry about *Face the People* because there was an early campaign breakfast meeting with volunteers and supporters, followed by a brunch meeting. She was so busy being on, smiling, talking, pleasing everyone, that she scarcely thought about the telecast until they were once again in the car en route.

In the studio itself, Tildy was relieved to find that she did not sit with Stephen this time. Nor was she to be introduced. The TV people, with assorted walkie-talkie equipment dangling from their necks, had everything planned. She and the other campaign people were seated in a glassed-in booth, where they could watch both the live show and view a TV receiving monitor.

Tildy was confident that she looked good in her simple apricot dress. From the Sacramento sun and the time spent here in southern California, she was beginning to get a creamy tan, which was very becoming. Her honey-toned hair was caught up at the back to show her graceful neck and chin line. She was glad that she was pleasing to look at because she was aware of plenty of attention. Cameras flashed at intervals—by whom, she did not know—so she sat slightly forward in her chair, trying to appear interested, unperturbed, and very confident in the candidate.

The program format was familiar, beginning on a very

friendly note, conveying an air of almost camaraderie to the viewing audience. It was odd watching behind the scenes, with the various television people crouched here and there out of camera range in front of the panel, murmuring their directions into tiny microphones, holding up printed cards, or making strange, alien gestures by way of silent instruction. On the small monitor set, Tildy saw the panel of four reporters and Stephen, all seated in an easy, relaxed manner in a semicircle. The program moved along rather quickly, an introduction of each panelist and the promise to introduce Stephen after a short break for a sponsor's message. But they had already started on him, because the promise of the coming introduction referred to Stephen Talbot as an unusually important Independent candidate and one of the richest men in California, possibly the nation.

Suddenly, after the commercial, in the very beginning of the program, Stephen was taking it away from them, taking the offensive. His magnetism came through on the monitor, almost as clearly as when her glance went from it to the live scene beyond the glass booth.

"Let's pursue that point," he was saying in a relaxed manner. "You mentioned the Talbot money. I was worried about that in the beginning—actually now I have found that it's not a liability at all with the thinking voters, the independents. I've talked to a lot of them and, on the whole, they seemed relieved that I have money of my own. They seem to think—and I concur—that the candidate who doesn't need money badly is less likely to wheel and deal for personal profit. I've been finding that being a rich man isn't at all the handicap some people thought it would be politically."

The subject was changed immediately. Tildy felt a thrill of excitement. He had taken the wind out of their sails on at least that issue.

Later he scored again.

Despite the fact that Stephen was obviously doing well, Tildy felt an increasing tension. She listened with painful intensity as he answered questions, parried them, or turned them to his own advantage. Despite her feeling of excitement and—oddly enough—pride, she was relieved when the program was over.

They returned as quickly as they could to the hotel. It was almost four o'clock and they hadn't had lunch, but they seemed of one mind. They wanted to analyze that telecast. Tildy felt a tingling of excitement. Without understanding too much about it, she knew that Stephen had done well, remarkably well, and that the campaign people were delighted about it. In the car there were snatches of comments regarding changes in plans. They would have the young people conduct another poll as soon as possible. They now needed to update data on Independents and undecideds. They planned to review their schedule of purchased television time to use later when the campaign peaked.

But back at the hotel, with first one tape recorder playing and then the other, on a table spread with papers and the remains of sandwiches and empty coffee cups, the glow began to tarnish for Tildy.

Jeremy Newman was saying almost feverishly, "Alan, run that part again. Now listen, Vera, that part about the 'thinking voter.' That's beautiful. You can use that in his speeches."

Alan interrupted excitedly, "And that part about the independent being tired of being used. Terrific!"

"Run it back again," Vera said. "No, further. Now. Stop. Where he says 'outmoded party system.' Good. Very good. And that 'served us well in its time.' Excellent. Now, Steve, next time why don't you add something like 'We must now move on' or 'move ahead' might be a better phrase. Just to lock in that idea."

Everyone was making notes.

Tildy shrank down farther in her chair, turning an empty coffee cup around in her hands. Talk about the voters being used. They were trying to use them, improvising, selecting, discarding, like a group of showmen. That's all it was, a big show!

And through it all Stephen sat there, listening to them

93

thoughtfully, intently, storing it all away in that tough, clever brain of his. Suddenly she had to get out! She got up from her chair.

But Stephen reached out and placed his hand on her arm. "Wait a moment," was all he said, but with such an underlying tone of command that she sat back down.

She swallowed, wanting to cry, hoping desperately that she wouldn't. *Oh, Stephen. You faker! You fraud!*

All during the telecast he had seemed so sincere, so real, so good, so right about it all. During any time in that brief, tense half-hour, she would have gone out and voted for him. More than that, she would have stood on the corner holding up a placard or handing out leaflets. Please vote for Stephen Talbot.

"We'll do two separate surveys," Vera was deciding. "I need one to judge the impact of this single telecast. Stephen, you were good today. This has done a lot for the campaign impetus. As of now, things will pick up speed. It's those undecideds we need to worry about. If we only knew which way they'll go inside the election booths." She sat back in her chair.

Tildy remained where she was. She was burningly aware of Stephen's hand, his light touch on her arm. He was holding her there, just as surely as if he were exerting an iron grip. She had not the faintest doubt that if she started to move before he wanted her to, he could—probably would—exert that grip. For some weird reason of his own he wanted her here beside him.

"Make copies of those tapes to send on to Marv." Vera was speaking again, and there was a kind of finishing motion, as if they had all decided that the meeting was— finally—over.

As they got up to go, Stephen turned to Tildy.

"I have a couple of things to discuss with you, Tildy." That was his command to her, and his dismissal to the others in case any felt inclined to stay on awhile. They put away the notes, and gathered up all the papers, leaving only the remains of their hasty sandwich lunch and empty coffee cups. How cautious they all were.

94

When they were finally alone, Tildy couldn't look at Stephen. She stood like a miserable child, wanting desperately to get away but not quite daring to go.

"All right, Tildy, what's troubling you? Let's get it out in the open."

"N-nothing. It doesn't matter. It's my problem."

"No, it isn't. Until November your problems are mine, too. You sat all through the meeting like the frozen snow princess, sending out icy waves of disapproval. Now, why?"

"All right!" she suddenly lashed out at him. "Because it's such a big lie. All of it! When you were on the broadcast, I thought you were just great. I was going along! I was believing!" She was almost crying and hated it. "And now, when it's over, all this cold-blooded analysis. Taking apart everything you said, every gesture you made, every time you frowned or laughed—making a big thing out of your every word. It's all so false. You're using everybody. You're planning to use the voters to get into office. Everything is calculated to convince somebody, to move somebody to do what you want them to do. I—" She stopped, and put one tight fist to her mouth. She was going to cry, and there was nothing she could do about it.

Stephen waited silently until the stormy weeping subsided and then—oh, damn—she couldn't even find a handkerchief or tissue. Oh, but he could. Even before he handed her his handkerchief, she knew he would. She wanted to ball it up and throw it at him but instead she took it, gulped back an hysterical laugh, and wiped her eyes.

"My—eye makeup," she gasped. "I—you'll have to excuse me!"

"Why don't you have a quick wash? I'll wait. Use my bathroom."

Snatching up her handbag, she escaped for the moment. So calm. As if he had all the time in the world. As if there were nothing at all pressing on him, surrounding him.

Deliberately, Tildy took her time washing her face, redoing her scanty makeup, and combing her hair. Let him wait. If he had to wait long enough, maybe he would go away.

He was standing casually at the french window when she returned.

"Feel better?" he asked conversationally. "Sometimes it takes a blowup to clear the air and release a bit of tension. When you blow, you really do a good job."

No anger? No disapproval?

She looked at him uncertainly.

"That's a nice pool out there," he said. "There's nobody in it, so I assume it's for the use of this cottage only. I think we should take a swim before dinner. Relax us both."

Tildy felt a sense of wariness.

"But first I do want to clarify a couple of points."

Ah, she thought, *here it comes,* and prepared herself to listen. A job was a job.

"First we have to go back to one of the points I tried to make with you before—we're in the middle of a battle. A battle means that there are adversaries, enemies, out there. Have you got that?"

"I understand that politics is a fight," she conceded.

"Then let's cover the point about how many millions of voters there are to be reached in California—this is the most populous state in the union, you know. Each one has to get my message."

"Yes, I know that."

"Okay, so far so good. You said that during the telecast you were convinced of my sincerity—do you know why?"

"You—you're a good showman?" She began to feel tentative.

"Maybe. But also because during that telecast I meant what I said. Maybe what you were hearing—what convinced you at that time—was the fact that I was speaking the simple truth."

She regarded him soberly, a tiny hope flickering in her mind.

"Then we get to the rough part, don't we?" he asked almost kindly. "The part about the analysis after the telecast, the part that offended you so. Vera, Alan, and Jeremy all sitting around the table listening and listening again and taking apart every word I said. And planning to use this and that again. Saying this word was good and that word wasn't. That's what gets to you, doesn't it?"

"Yes, it's so contrived. So calculated."

"It is." Momentarily there was a kind of sadness in his face, and then it was bland again, as if his guard had been down for a moment but was no longer. "But in a battle doesn't one have to contrive and calculate? Because there is always another battle coming, always many more battles. Then it helps the fighters to analyze their individual battles to see what worked and what didn't. Every tiny thing you do in a battle that is right, that gets results, obtains an advantage, you will want to repeat in the next one to increase the results and magnify the benefit. Don't you understand that? I told you in the beginning that I have to play the game by the existing rules—whether I like them or not—or I'm out of the game before I begin."

He came to stand before her, taking her shoulders in his hands. She tried to steel herself against her reaction to those strong hands.

"You must believe me when I tell you that I said those words honestly. I meant them. The fact that later the professionals took over and began to dissect it all, I cannot fault. That's their job, Tildy—to help me win this election. They do this purely and simply by having me stress and repeat everything I do that is effective. That's the way it is, Tildy. It just comes down to basic common sense. And one way or another you'll have to live with it until November." Now he did take away his hands, and perversely this annoyed her. "Would you like a swim?"

"Yes," she said fervently. Leisure. Slow swimming up and down in the lovely pool. Thinking about nothing more demanding than how blue the water was, how green the spreading lawns, how vivid the massed shrubbery.

The water seemed actually a kind of turquoise, with millions of ripples because Stephen was already swimming with exquisite precision up and down the length of it when she came out in her swimsuit. Surrounding the pool was an irregular paving of pastel-colored flagstones. She wondered what shale cliffs in California had yielded up these slabs of pale beige, peach, lavender, and gray. They all blended crookedly with the velvety green lawns, beyond which were heavy masses of red, tangerine, and yellow hibiscus.

Savoring the moment, she stood on the tip of the diving board. She had longed to wear this swimsuit since the day she had paid an outrageous price for it from Stephen's money. It was beautifully made, clinging to her slim, curving body. The salesgirl had called the color nude but it was actually a pale, pinkish beige.

Then she dived in, cutting the water cleanly, loving it, momentarily shocked by the coldness, then becoming accustomed to it. She surfaced and began a lazy crawl toward the far end. Stephen was at the side now, holding to the ladder, not even watching her—for a change. His head was back, eyes closed, the sun coming down on his face and strong throat.

Oh, this was good.

For quite a while it seemed that each was alone. She became more aware of him again when she started to tire. She had forgotten to count how many laps she had done but it really didn't matter. She let herself drift to a stop near the center of the pool and stayed there a few minutes, treading water. The warm quiet peace of the sun-drenched afternoon settled over her. The rest of the vast hotel seemed a thousand miles away, they were so sheltered here.

"Why don't you come out and rest awhile?" Stephen asked, now clinging again lazily to the ladder.

"All right, in a minute." She watched him turn and go up, pondering that this was the first time she had seen him in swim trunks. They were low, hip hugging, some kind of white knit that clung to his tanned, muscular body. She floated dreamily, thinking that he really should have been a model in an art class.

"Are you coming?" He was out now, standing there, water running off him, observing her.

"Yes." May as well give up and follow. Slowly, she drifted to the side and climbed out. On the warm flagstones there was a square of blue canvas, wide enough for two people, stretched on a metal frame above the paving—a kind of stationary hammock.

"Here, it's not too bright over here. We can stretch out a few minutes before we go in to change for dinner." Stephen said stretching out his own tall broad-shouldered body on the far side of it. He was right, this was one of the few places by the pool which was in dappled sun and shade, not all the blinding glare. She lay down and stretched luxuriously. She was still a bit breathless from her swim.

She started to say something to Stephen and glanced over at him. His heavily lashed eyes were closed, and his breathing even. Could he be asleep so quickly? She decided to keep quiet, just in case. He had had a demanding day; let him rest.

She almost dozed off herself. There was something lulling and drowsy in the too warm southern California sunlight that seemed to permeate the body and melt the bones into limpness. The early Mexican settlers here had been right; the afternoon siesta was a divine institution, to be faithfully observed. She began to ease into that floating state between sleeping and waking when she became vaguely aware that Stephen had moved beside her.

"Are you asleep?" he asked softly.

"No," she said drowsily, "not very."

He laughed softly. "Not very. What does that mean? Oh, Tildy." He moved closer and was somehow over her. "Have you the least idea how lovely you are?"

It seemed everything was in very slow motion. It seemed—surely she must be asleep—that he was going to kiss her again. There weren't any reporters or cameras or public to see. She struggled into full wakefulness as his mouth came down slowly on hers, moving gently, enticing, then demanding, her response. She gave it. The familiar slow, molten heat moved inside her and without volition her arms encircled his broad, brown shoulders, clinging to him, pressing him downward.

Then he was pulling away, deliberately, relentlessly.

"Tildy," he said huskily. "I'm sorry. I'm afraid I'm as susceptible as the next guy. But we can't allow any emotional involvement."

She lay there, wordless. Any emotional involvement! What was he talking about—emotional involvement! She was so emotionally involved, she couldn't think straight. All he had to do was touch her and she melted. She wanted to cry.

There was a movement in the shrubbery across the pool.

"Damn," Stephen said in a low tone.

"What is it?" Her voice was unsteady.

"Someone. I don't know if it was part of the press or not. He had a camera."

Oh no, not a camera this time. She was desperate to believe that Stephen hadn't known about the camera. Oh, please.

CHAPTER 11

They were back in Sacramento Wednesday evening for a brief rest before starting out again mid-Friday, with demanding weekend commitments. Tildy went into her small apartment and shut the door behind her. It took her the better part of an hour to relax—the pace had been so hectic.

"I'm keeping a scrapbook of your pictures, Tildy." Uncle James had said happily one night on the telephone. "You know, from the newspapers, dear." A little, bright spot. She wondered hurriedly in passing what she would have done without those nightly telephone conversations with Uncle James.

She tried to put the whole campaign out of her mind. It was useless, she couldn't escape the last few days—the anxious discussions of this poll or that survey, of how many Independents there were now, of the marked increase in the undecideds. This did indicate that Stephen was making inroads among the registered Democrats and Republicans.

And underneath his calm Talbot exterior, she had sensed a growing tension. Once Stephen had been in sharp dispute with Lennie Bishop, his finance and funding chairman. Tildy had caught a fragment of conversation between the two men.

101

"Well, Stephen, the money is going too fast. We have to have more. That's final."

"And I said we cannot have any from the Talbot Foundation. The Foundation has nothing to do with politics—even mine!"

"Well, talk to that man Hallett again—he wants to contribute."

"No! He's a developer. As soon as I was in the Senate, he'd be after me to back his resort development in the mountains—I know what he wants, Lennie."

"But he's willing to change his resort plan. You could at least talk to him again. We're contracting for paid TV commercials now and that costs money."

That was all she had heard.

Now her own telephone rang. She let the bell sound four times before getting up reluctantly from the couch to answer it.

It was Stephen.

"Tildy, I'm sorry to spring this on you at the last minute, but my mother wants us to go to a reception tonight. It's the public engagement announcement."

A blaze of anger swept through her. This was her own free time! He had said so!

"Tildy? Are you there? I am sorry about this. Mother swears she told one of the aides about tonight, but somehow the message didn't get through. Incidentally, your uncle will be there. That should please you."

"Uncle James?" She was stunned, then alarmed, then fiercely protective. She could not imagine Uncle James attending any Talbot social function. There was a moment of stark dread—he didn't have a decent suit of clothes to his name!

"Yes, he was delighted. Incidentally," there was laughter running through Stephen's voice, "he told Mother he was going to vote for me. That pleased everybody, of course. I'll pick you up about six. We should be a bit early so we can visit with the family before the guests start to arrive."

"All right," Tildy said somewhat grimly.

When Stephen came to pick her up she knew she looked

102

good enough for the Talbots. She was wearing a long skirt of very thin, whisper-soft embroidered cotton, with a lacy, old-fashioned top. The skirt and top were white with cream-colored embroidery. This creamy white against her golden skin looked better than she had hoped. She had completed the look by tying a cream-colored velvet ribbon about her throat and hanging from it a golden pendant, which had once been her mother's. She had taken special pains with her fair hair, catching it up at the back, with a few wispy tendrils about the face and the nape of the neck.

"Good!" Stephen said when he saw her, and then, "What's the matter? Don't look so grim, Tildy. I know you're tired, but everything's going to be fine. Your uncle had arrived when I left. He and I took to each other right away."

Tildy was more intimidated than ever in behalf of Uncle James when she saw the Talbot home. It covered several levels on the slopes of rolling hills, looking as if it had been there since the time of the Spaniards. Here and there, seemingly without design, were terraces, gardens, and arbors, the entire effect harmonious, restful, and mellow. The huge front door was splendid, made of heavy, etched glass sheltered behind twisting wrought iron.

There was—oh, no!—a butler. Tildy had never seen a real live butler before in her life. This one was a tall, sandy-haired, middle-aged man who spoke directly to Stephen.

"Mr. Stephen, would you and Miss Marshall go into the library? Mr. Talbot wishes to see you."

"Certainly. Thanks, Crandall. This way, Tildy. It's back here."

Tildy was somewhat awestruck. The library was a gigantic room, two stories high. It made Stephen's personal library in his apartment look like a miniature. She longed for the chance to browse among the thousands of books. Surely they must all be cataloged. She wondered who took care of cataloging the new ones that he must add from time to time.

"Oh, there you are. Come in. How are you, Tildy?" Mr. Talbot was saying. "Forgive me if I don't get up."

"Certainly," Tildy murmured, trying not to show her quick sympathy to this formerly strong man who was now, very obviously, in pain.

"I'm not going to be able to stay down for the reception tonight, Stephen. You and Bruce will have to handle it with your mother. I will come down for the actual announcement and then go back up."

"Bruce and I can handle it," Stephen said, looking at his father intently. There was evidently a strong bond between them.

Then Tildy noticed for the first time that her Uncle James was there. She crossed the room to him quickly and kissed his cheek. "You look gorgeous," she managed to whisper, with a catch in her throat.

From somewhere—rented, no doubt—he had obtained a rather good-looking tuxedo. Then she realized that he had not responded to her and there was an uneasy flush to his usually pallid face. He looked taut and pinched.

Stephen's father was speaking again. "We've had some rather disturbing news. Apparently your campaign people haven't had word of it yet. A Mr.—er—Mr. Mason, one of the press people, was kind enough to hand this along to me."

Spread out on the wide, polished table was a sleazy tabloid-sized newspaper, the kind Tildy had seen in racks in the supermarkets and newsstands. It was a small weekly scandal sheet that published the most outrageous stories it could find for shock value only, with little attention to accuracy.

For this there was no story, just a picture with a caption. It said: "ON THE CAMPAIGN TRAIL. Stephen Talbot and campaign aide relax between speeches to church groups in southern California." That was all. Above it was a picture of Stephen kissing Tildy. The picture had been cropped in such a way that they both appeared naked. All the surrounding area, which might place them in any location or setting, had been eliminated. Stephen's bare back and Tildy's arms and shoulders, as well as the sides of their faces were clearly visible.

There was a long silence in the room.

"It looks bad, doesn't it, Stephen? Do you recall the—er—situation?" Mr. Talbot asked.

"Yes," Stephen said in his too calm voice. "It was by the swimming pool in that hotel where we all stayed in a garden cottage. Tildy was wearing a swimsuit and I was wearing trunks. Do you remember, Tildy? I told you I'd seen a man with a camera."

"Yes, I remember," she said woodenly, her face flaming.

"I'm afraid I offended Mr. Treadwell, Tildy's uncle. I jumped to the wrong conclusion. At first I didn't recognize the girl as Tildy, and Mr. Treadwell did recognize her immediately, of course. I certainly apologize."

"Are you apologizing to my niece?" Uncle James said clearly, his color still high.

"Uncle James," Tildy moaned desperately.

"Of course I am," Mr. Talbot said, with a slight bow in Tildy's direction. And my son will also, for having put her in such a position in the first place," he added.

Astounded, Tildy realized that he meant Stephen, the candidate. Oh, dear God, let the floor open up and swallow her. How could he apologize when she had clung to him, on fire with her response to him.

Without a flicker of expression in his eyes, Stephen turned to her.

"Please accept my apologies, Tildy. Your uncle has every right to be angry." He turned to Uncle James. "I hope you will also forgive me, sir. This was entirely my fault. It will never happen again."

Uncle James bowed stiffly.

She wanted to know—then dreaded ever knowing—what he had said to them in her defense, here in their spreading hillside mansion in his rented suit. Poor, darling, loyal, frail Uncle James, with the body of a sparrow and the heart of a lion. She realized for the first time that her head was aching, and suddenly she started to cry.

This focused everyone's attention on her, which seemed

to relieve them all somewhat. Uncle James was patting her on the shoulder. Mr. Talbot looked sorrowful, worried, and sick. Mrs. Talbot pressed a soft linen handkerchief into her hand.

"Come, Tildy dear," she said. "You will want to freshen up a bit. There is a powder room just off the library here."

Through it all, until Tildy had regained her composure, Stephen had remained as silent and motionless as a stone, not betraying the faintest glimmer of emotion.

In the small powder room she carefully did one thing at a time, concentrating on each. When her makeup was repaired, she stood a moment longer, looking at her reflection. Within the next few moments no one would be able to tell she had been crying. She felt a hardening of her will. Minute by minute she would go through the whole evening. She would not let Stephen down. She would not let Uncle James down. Somehow she would go through the receiving line, along with Mrs. Talbot. She would smile incessantly and say all the right things, go through the announcement of the phony engagement, accept all the good wishes and congratulations. Pretend. Pretend. Pretend. Then later in the evening, when she was partially free, she would—somehow—find a few moments to talk to Uncle James alone. Public figures belong to the public.

Just outside the library door was Chuck Mason, the lean, dark reporter she feared. He looked more stooped than usual, and Tildy noticed for the first time the tired lines about his eyes, which had seen too much, perhaps, of the ugly things in life.

"Tildy, wait up a minute." His hand touched her arm lightly.

"Yes?" She stopped, poised, her face blank.

"That in there—" He gestured back toward the library. "That isn't journalism, Tildy. I hope you realize that. And I didn't show it to old man Talbot just to be mean. In this game you have to know the worst so you can be prepared. You understand?"

"Yes," she said. "I understand. And thanks."

"Incidentally, when there is time I'd like to mention

something to you—you might want to pass it on to the candidate. He's made a couple of goofs in his speeches. His opponents are going to make hay out of it."

She stood stock still. Stephen making mistakes—it hardly seemed possible. "We must talk about it later," she murmured, hurrying along to join Mrs. Talbot.

For the next several hours she was swept along in the pattern of the evening. It was unreal, like a stately pavane in a golden, hazy dream, with the sound of tinkling laughter and tinkling glasses around the edges.

She was being publicly presented as Stephen Talbot's fiancée. There were several hundred people here to see it and come to her smiling and laughing, saying pleasant things. One smiling face blended into another as the evening wore on.

During the announcement itself, she almost felt as if she were standing aside watching a play: Stephen, laughing, holding her close to his side, his other arm upraised, holding his champagne glass; she, smiling radiantly; Mr. Talbot by the massive fireplace, leaning heavily on his cane; Mrs. Talbot being Mrs. Talbot, perfect in every expression; Uncle James, near the doorway, trying to smile and not quite making it.

She got through it all right and gradually the excitement from the announcement subsided and the pattern of the reception asserted itself again.

Some time later Chuck Mason confronted her amid the eddying crowd.

"Look, babe, I'll say this quickly because I know you are on display and your time isn't your own."

"What is it?" She gave him her most charming mechanical smile.

"It's your boyfriend, Golden Boy Candidate and the mistakes he made yesterday—one in each speech."

"He couldn't have," Tildy said sharply, then smiled to cover it up because two people turned to look at her.

"Keep it down, babe. I'm telling you—and you can get the word to him if you want to—and I think you should—that Mr. Invincible misquoted his Republican opponent

107

yesterday on tax reform. He also misquoted his Democratic opponent on full-time students collecting unemployment insurance."

"Misquoted?"

"Yep," Mason said, in his wise and weary way. "I'm an old political pro, Tildy, and I know what those guys said, and I know what Golden Boy said they said—and it's not the same. Somebody better check it out." He drifted away in the crowd and she turned automatically to reply to someone else who was speaking to her. It couldn't be! Stephen wouldn't make mistakes like that!

"Tildy?" Uncle James was beside her holding a glass of champagne. He was smiling, but his eyes were troubled. "Is there any place we can talk a few moments?"

"Yes, of course," She took his arm, trying not to clutch it like a little girl. "I'm not sure of the way the house is laid out—"

"This way," he murmured. "Let's drift toward that door." His eyes had begun to twinkle. "I admit it's a problem. There is a room in that direction where Mrs. Talbot keeps some of her Indian relics in display cases. She showed them to me earlier."

"Stephen mentioned that she has made herself something of an authority."

"She is, Tildy. Her collection is fascinating. She's invited me to stay on for a few days—here's the door. Slip right in here."

Like a couple of conspirators they slid inside the room and shut the door. The room was massive, with many glass display cases and wall racks upon which hung Indian costumes and ritual paraphernalia.

"Tildy dear," Uncle James said gently. "There's no time to look at anything now—tempting as it is. I have to ask you this—" He paused, his eyes now troubled. "Are you getting into this too deeply? I understand that it is—" He shrugged, somehow letting her know that he realized that it was all make-believe, and that he understood. "You are doing this for me, Tildy. And it occurred to me tonight, when that nasty tabloid was brought to our attention, that perhaps you are getting in too deep. Perhaps this was all

108

a mistake—a generous one on your part, my dear, but a mistake all the same."

"But, Uncle James, even if it is a mistake—what can I do now? Mrs. Talbot has just announced the engagement. Do you realize that if I leave now, it might ruin Stephen's chances. Don't you see? Just think what the press would do with it."

He regarded her thoughtfully. "Tildy, are you going to be hurt by this charade?"

She waited a long moment before she answered, knowing it had to be the truth. Then she said, "I don't know. I think so." There was a stubborn line to her jaw.

"I think so, too," he said sadly.

"I have to go through with it." She was startled at the hard sound of her voice.

"Why, Tildy?" His voice was very quiet.

They stared at each other and Tildy said it in her mind for the first time: *I'm in love with him.* Uncle James read it in her eyes.

"Oh, my dear child," he murmured. "Is there anything I can say to—"

"Nothing." Again she was amazed at the quality of her voice. It was utterly implacable. "I am going to see this through. You don't have to worry about the ending." She would not let her voice break. "The ending is all arranged. The whole thing will be over the day after the election— win or lose. It has been agreed between us, Stephen and me. I will issue a statement that the engagement is terminated and," she ended bleakly, "Vera Briggs will probably write my statement."

There was a long, sad silence between them.

"It's only until November," she said when she could stand the silence no longer.

"Yes."

"Uncle James? Are you going to stay on here for a few days?"

"No, dear. I think not. I'm obligated to stay tonight, but I'll leave tomorrow morning."

"This is not the end of the world, you know. I've had

disappointments before. I just—hadn't counted on this part of it."

"I understand." Desperately they both sought for something else to say to break the pall that hung over them. Tildy noticed for the first time that Uncle James's rented suit was slightly too wide for his frail shoulders, and he was noticing the shimmer to her gray eyes, as if tears were very close again.

"Well," he said briskly, "we can thank that chap, Mason, for enlightening me on the various types of journalism."

"Mason?" Tildy asked vaguely.

"Yes. He took me aside awhile ago and explained to me exactly how that picture could have been cropped to make it look so suggestive. Nice fellow."

The door opened suddenly and they both turned, saved from any further effort at conversation. It was Stephen.

"So this is where you disappeared to, Tildy. Oh, hello, sir. Don't mean to intrude, but people are starting to leave and mother thought Tildy should—"

"Of course," Tildy said hastily. She gave Uncle James's arm a parting squeeze. In just ten seconds flat, no matter how she felt inside, she was going to be standing in that mass of people again, turning this way and that, smiling and smiling. This was what she had agreed to do, and do it she would.

The crowd finally thinned out to a few longtime friends of the Talbots and Tildy found herself momentarily alone. She looked around for Uncle James but failed to see him. He had looked increasingly tired as the evening had progressed. Stephen was nowhere to be seen either, and she began to think with longing of the little apartment across town. Soon, very soon now, Stephen would appear and say they were leaving, and she would tell Mrs. Talbot good night and thank her for a lovely evening. Some day—for some other girl—this would all be real. That lovely gracious lady would give another reception to announce the real engagement; or more likely, the girl's parents would be doing it. Tildy was more tired than she had realized and leaned against the back of a tall velvet chair by a fireplace. Where was Stephen?

She had better start looking for him before she fell over and went to sleep like the dormouse at the tea party. She got as far as the main hallway when she encountered two people leaving. The butler was just opening the door for them, bowing slightly. Tildy's mind groped for their names.

"Mr. and Mrs. Hallett, are you leaving us so soon?" Automatically, she extended her hand.

"Yes, my dear," Mrs. Hallett was saying, "Walter has an appointment in the morning in Seattle. And he really must get some rest."

"Let me wish you every happiness," Mr. Hallett was saying. "That Stephen Talbot is a lucky fellow."

When the door closed behind them, Tildy started toward the library in the rear. The Halletts had come from that direction. She was right. Before she reached the library door she could hear Stephen's voice. It sounded relieved, with a kind of pleased excitement.

"Thank God Lennie persisted until I talked to Hallett again. Just look at that. Isn't that great!"

"It is, just great. And poor Hallett wanted so badly to contribute something. Now you can accept with a clear conscience."

Tildy stopped suddenly. The other voice was Vera's. She wondered who else was with them and went toward the door again. They were alone.

Stephen had spread out on the massive table what appeared to be plans or drawings of some sort. His arms, spread out, were holding down the farthest edges, which attempted to curl up, as if they had been in a roll. Vera stood close to him, her hand on his shoulder, clinging almost. So unlike Vera.

"Look, Vera, all that virgin timber not to be touched, not one tree goes. And see here, this valley. The surveyors' reports show it almost level—perfect for camp grounds. And there are three places like that. Then over here, only one area is to be developed, and most of that was burned out by a forest fire three years ago."

"And did you see the sketches by the architects for the lodge and village? Steve, it's so beautiful."

111

"I can hardly believe that Hallett would come up with something like this. You'd think he was the original conservationist, he's so cautious about cutting down trees or changing a stream course." He was half-laughing and so was she. There seemed something soft, gentle, and womanly about her face at this moment. She was really quite attractive. The chilly, frosty Vera was gone. This was a woman in love. In a minute Stephen, so absorbed at the moment in the plans, would notice it.

"I can't tell you how grateful I am that you persisted in this," Stephen was saying. "Lennie will be delighted."

"I know," Vera was laughing softly, her hand still clinging to his shoulder.

"I could kiss you," Stephen said absently, still intent on the plans.

"Why don't you?" she asked and he glanced up, surprised. He had lifted one hand and the large sheets of paper started to roll up briskly. It was heavy stiff paper. The roll bumped his other hand. An odd silence stretched out and Vera melted against him, her arms sliding around his neck.

Tildy watched, fascinated, repelled, as he lowered his head and his mouth met hers. His arms went around her and he held her against his body.

Blindly, Tildy turned away.

CHAPTER 12

When she left with Stephen some time later, Mrs. Talbot blew her a kiss from the door. Tildy was oddly touched, and the fanlight over the doorway shimmered. That meant she had tears in his eyes. She turned quickly and went down the broad, shallow steps just ahead of Stephen. His cream-colored Jaguar stood on the white-graveled drive, its motor running.

Inside, she lay back against the leather seat, slowly beginning to let go, to relax,. Her evening performance was over. Soon now she would be in her own little apartment. There was one more thing she had to do. What was it? She began wearily to sort out the crowded recollections of the evening.

"I had some good news tonight," Stephen said, breaking into her thoughts.

"Oh, I'm glad," she said pleasantly. "What was it?"

"I learned that it's okay to accept a contribution from Walter Hallett—you know, that Seattle real estate developer who wants to build a resort in the California mountains."

"Yes, I met him. Lennie will be glad to get the money." She wondered what was different about Stephen's voice. It sounded slightly strained, as if he were just making polite conversation.

She sat up suddenly. "Stephen, I have to tell you something."

"What is it?"

"Chuck Mason spoke to me this evening. He says that two mistakes have occurred in your speeches. He said that something must be wrong in the organization."

She could see his profile against a lighted sign they passed. It was grim.

"I know. Something is wrong."

"You know!"

"I just found out this evening. What did Mason say to you?"

"That you misquoted your opponents on tax reform and students receiving unemployment benefits. I can't remember exactly what you said—"

"I can. I know just what he means." He was silent a moment. "That was decent of Mason to mention it."

"What are you going to do? Why did these mistakes happen? Were you too tired—driving yourself too hard?"

He pulled the car to a stop in front of her apartment house. "They happened because somebody made them happen," he said evenly, taking the key from the ignition. "That occurs in political campaigns, Tildy. It's known as dirty tricks. There are people working in the campaigns who devise ways to embarrass the other candidates when they can. Sometimes they even infiltrate another candidate's organization. It's done all the time. My popularity has gone up considerably since that nationwide telecast. We knew that our opponents were getting worried—they think I'll drain off too many votes from them." He sat back against the seat a moment, holding the keys in his strong hand. "It's a miserable game."

"What are you going to do?"

"I'm going to continue campaigning up into northern California, Fort Bragg on Friday. Two speeches in Eureka on Saturday. We're going almost to the Oregon border. Then Monday, coming back down through Mendocino, we stop off and meet a filming crew to make some TV commercials for use later in the campaign. They'll take

114

a lot of still pictures, too. I want you in most of them with me."

"I mean about the mistakes. What are you going to do about that?"

"Apologize publicly to my opponents. I've already talked to each candidate on the phone this evening. My private apologies to them were accepted. All very good-humoredly. They know the score."

"But they will bring it up in their speeches? Use it against you?"

"You bet they will."

"And—that's all?"

"No." Despite the edge of fatigue that sounded in his voice there was that other sound she recognized, that low steely quality. "We have to find out who in our staff is planting phony information for Vera to use in my speeches."

"You mean it could happen again?"

"Until we find out who is responsible, and get rid of him or her. It could be anybody who has access to the Sacramento office. Vera has talked to Marv about it. They're both working on it. Come on, let me take you upstairs. You look beat."

At her doorway, she turned suddenly to him.

"I'm sorry," she said impulsively. "I'm sorry that they—that somebody—is trying to—to spoil things. I—"

What had a woman done a million years ago when she sensed her mate was in danger? The errant idea made her smile wistfully. Stephen was looking at her with an expression she could not place for a moment. Measuring? Calculating?

"You're a good little campaigner," he said remotely. "I'd hate to lose you. Give me your key and I'll open the door."

Inside the apartment he said, still in that carefully controlled tone, "I know you're tired, but there is something I want to ask you about. Then I'll leave." He was looking at her steadily. "I have to ask it, you understand. We have a business arrangement to maintain and that can only be done with mutual confidence."

115

She didn't understand what he meant.

"I managed to take a little time this evening to talk to some of the key people. They are upset that someone has infiltrated the campaign, or been reached by the opposition in some way." He paused. "It isn't you, is it?"

For a moment she didn't really grasp what he had said. When she did, she couldn't answer, simply stared at him wordlessly, all color draining from her face. Then blindly she turned and started across the room to her bedroom.

She knew he was after her before she felt his hands. They were inside the bedroom now. As helplessly as a puppet, she was whirled around to face him, his strong hands gripping her upper arms.

"You didn't answer me." It was that hard, toneless quality in his voice that she hated. She twisted in his grasp.

"Who even suggested that I am responsible!" Anger was beginning to beat in the back of her head. She thought, *How dare they! How dare they!*

"We went over the list of names of people who work, or have worked, in the Sacramento office—Vera gets her data through that office."

"I don't care a damn where Vera gets her data—" She was trying to twist away, pushing against his chest.

"It was pointed out that there had been no trouble before you came."

"Of all the despicable—" She almost broke away, but he slammed her against the dresser and held her there with his body.

"And it was you who released the engagement story prematurely to the press, locking yourself into the campaign."

"Let me go! You have no right—" Her head was reeling with the intensity of her emotion.

"I have every right! Now, answer me!"

"I won't! I won't dignify—"

"You have no money. Do you want money? Did they offer you money? What did you do? Did somebody reach you? Did you sell out!"

"No!" she screamed, appalled. "No, I did not. No!

116

Never. I wouldn't do such a thing!" She was anguished, outraged, terrified, all at once.

"Be quiet." His voice grated. "Keep your voice down."

She sagged against him, hopeless, helpless, because he didn't believe her. His face was like granite, his eyes like chips of stone.

Slowly he released her and she leaned against the dresser, her legs weak. A weary panic flickered through her mind. She had to defend herself. How could she convince him? Her mouth was dry.

"You—investigated me so thoroughly," she said weakly. "Surely you remember all those tests I took. You said I was honest. You said I was loyal. Surely you must know—" She stopped, unable to go on.

He was looking at her thoughtfully. "I would be inclined to believe you, Tildy," he said finally. "How much money do you have? Right now?"

She looked at him blankly before she understood. He was going to check it out. Ruthlessly, relentlessly, he would follow through until it was proved to his satisfaction that she had no money he could not account for. Her purse was on the floor just inside the bedroom door where she had dropped it. She gestured toward it.

"I have all the money left from the clothing money you gave me. I have last week's pay check. I didn't cash it. I was going to put it in the bank," she explained dully. "There is about—I think—ten dollars in cash. And—and—I don't have anything else. Except maybe twenty or so left in my checking account at Wells Fargo in San Francisco."

"All right, I do believe you." But he picked up the purse anyway, and verified what she had said. She watched him distantly, seeming outside herself, as if she were watching some people on the stage. Maybe this was a kind of shock. She had nothing in any bank beyond the small checking account. But he would have his organization run through a credit check on her to see if any new account had been opened in any other bank. He was very thorough.

"Thank you, Tildy," he said. He sounded courteous,

117

impersonal. "I told the others I thought we could count on your loyalty. But you understand that everything has to be looked into."

She nodded wordlessly.

After he had gone, Tildy stood a long time, leaning limply against the dresser in her elegant, embroidered gown, trying to determine her feelings. Anger? Humiliation? Sorrow? Love?

Did she really love that man?

She could still feel the weight and strength of his body against hers. Was that love? Was this all there was to it, this primitive animal need, this deep physical hungering? Could she really love a man who didn't trust her, who didn't care two pins whether she lived or died, who was using her briefly to further his own ambition and would throw her away without a second thought when he needed her no longer. Uncle James didn't know how right he had been when he had thought she was going to be hurt. Before this ruthless man got through with her, he would break her heart. She straightened up slightly. She hoped—oh, how she hoped—that he would not break her pride, too. At least let her walk out of his life with that much left.

Monday they joined the filming crew in Mendocino. She found that Vera had prepared a script for them for a TV commercial to be used later in the campaign. Tildy studied it in her motel room at night. When she put it down, she consciously relaxed her lips, which had been in a cynical smile.

At breakfast Vera spoke to them crisply. "I remembered those haunting pictures of John Kennedy on that lonely beach at Hyannis. Very effective. They've been shown and repeated everywhere. We're going to do something like that for Steve."

Back in her motel room, Tildy changed to the clothing Vera had directed her to bring along—jeans, a light cotton blouse, sandals, a bandana. She had finished when there was a rap on the door. It was Stephen.

"I'm just ready," she said, wondering somewhat nervously if she had taken too long. It seemed odd to see him so casually dressed. He, too, was wearing jeans and a faded shirt, open at the throat.

"No hurry. I'm early. I wanted to speak to you a moment."

"Of course," she murmured, opening the door wider and letting him in. Now what?

"You're brooding about the other night at your apartment, aren't you?" he asked without preamble. His voice was calm and impersonal. "That won't do, Tildy. I have to protect this candidacy. I have to protect myself. Wherever there is a question, I have to find the answer. You must accept that."

"Did—did you find it?" Tildy asked.

"Yes, I did," he said frankly. "You are absolutely clear."

She waited for a sense of relief, but it did not come—only a further sense of withdrawal because he had not believed her, he had had to verify everything. She waited a moment for him to apologize. That did not come either. As he had said, he had a right to protect himself.

"Well, then," she said lamely. "I guess that's over."

"Is it?"

"What do you mean?"

"I don't know if the others have sensed it or not, but the disapproving snow princess is back again. You've withdrawn behind that cold barricade."

"Wh-what did you expect me to do? No one has ever doubted my word before—"

"I tried to explain in the beginning that this a rough game. You agreed to play."

"I am! I'm here, aren't I? I didn't walk out!"

"Yes, but you are supposed to be my loving fiancée, remember? And we're going down on that Mendocino beach now and make a TV commercial in which we are investing thousands of dollars. We're going to take a lot of still pictures, too, separately and together. This icy withdrawal of yours will come through, Tildy. The camera is relentless. Your job is to portray a woman in love with me."

119

"I—I'll do it," Tildy said uncertainly. What was he getting at?

"Feeling the way you do, I don't think you can, Tildy. Maybe it's that great honesty you're supposed to have. However, no matter what you think of me personally—and I don't want to know what it is—you do respond to me physically. As they say, the chemistry is right. And when we go down on that beach, I want you to look as if you're crazy about me. Do you understand?"

"N-no, I guess I don't," she said, looking at him blankly. As soon as she said it, she did understand. There was a moment of stark disbelief as he came toward her.

"Oh, no, don't," she gasped. Turning, she stumbled against her still unmade bed, and would have fallen except that he caught her. He twisted her around and held her against him. Iron fingers clamped under her jaw, lifting her face. It was a long, angry, brutal kiss. He pushed her down on the bed and held her there.

"Stop it, Tildy. Be still. I'm not going to let you go." His voice was deadly calm.

She stopped struggling, staring up at him He meant it. Trying to resist him was useless—she had not one half his strength. All right, she thought, it wouldn't make any difference. She hated him when he was arrogant like this. Deliberately, she went limp. He sat down on the side of the bed and pulled her limp form up into his arms. He wanted to melt the snow princess, did he? Let him try!

Expertly, carefully, as if he had all the time in the world, he started kissing her. Her lips parted, she couldn't help it. Slow panic started to build in her as she felt herself responding. She stiffened, twisted, trying to resist him, but she could not. The slow, langorous hunger was awakened again by his demanding mouth, the heat of his hands on her body. Unable to quell her response, her hands clung to his shoulders, caressing his back, pressing him down closer. She was clinging to him desperately, hungry for him, her lips seeking his again and again. How long it lasted she had no idea, but when he started to pull away

120

she clung to him. He forced her back down on the disheveled bed. She lay there, her heart pounding, her breath coming in sobbing gasps. He got up and stood looking down at her.

"Now," he said, "now you look like a woman in love." His tone told her nothing. Whatever he felt—if anything—was hidden.

She turned and buried her burning face in the pillow.

"Come on, Tildy. Let's go." He reached down and pulled her up, dragging her off the bed.

"Let me go," she moaned. Then, when she knew he wouldn't, she pleaded, "Wait—just give me a minute."

"Of course." He stood there, waiting as she struggled to button her blouse, and stuff it back under the waistband of her jeans. She stumbled into the bathroom and washed her face in cold water. When she tried to repair her makeup, her hands shook. He came and stood behind her. He was too close, too close. In a kind of panic, she half-turned.

"Finish what you're doing," he commanded calmly. "Look at yourself. That's the girl I want in the pictures. Look how wide and dark your eyes are. Look how soft and tender your mouth is. No, leave your hair alone. We want it tumbled like that. You're just right. Now, come on." He took hold of her shaking hand and pulled her outside the motel door, shutting it behind them. She felt vulnerable, exposed, knowing her feelings for him were clearly visible to anyone who cared to look. And beneath the shock in her mind, beneath the mingled humiliation and resentment, there was a crazy feeling of dark delight that he had so humbled her, forced her to bend to his will. She stumbled a little coming toward the waiting group of people and his arm went around her to steady her.

"Vera and the film crew are already set up down on the beach," Alan was saying.

Docilely she walked along beside Stephen, her heart thudding. She felt a kind of wry amusement at herself, at her appalling situation.

It was a chilly day, and the mist hung over the rocks and crags of the steep descent to the strip of driftwood-strewn beach. It was hard going. She was violently aware of Stephen's hands on her body as he helped her down the steep path of the bluff.

She was beginning to feel the cold. Maybe it would soothe and cool her unruly, traitorous body.

Vera was waiting for them with the crew. She had the site selected and the crew had set up their equipment. Tildy found with relief that they would work with just Stephen for a while, not needing her yet.

She huddled on a craggy outcropping of rock on the beach, one foot resting on an ancient piece of driftwood, with which the long beach was scattered from the restless tides. The hard-packed sand gleamed wetly.

The film crew was competent and businesslike. From time to time she was summoned for still pictures, alone or with Stephen, posing on the driftwood, climbing over gigantic rock formations, surrounded by the swirling, whispering foam as the waves came and went among the chinks and crannies of the rocks, her hair blowing in the wind.

They worked all day, stopping briefly for a sandwich lunch and, from time to time, hot coffee. Stephen was good. He knew all his lines. She had none. She was just part of the background.

That evening in their conference room in the motel, they watched the rushes of the day's motion picture filming. They were seated in deep lounge chairs in the darkened room, warm and well-fed, sipping excellent brandy from bubble-thin glasses. The films were all acceptable. No retakes were necessary. Later they would be spliced together for proper continuity. Stephen's brief messages, delivered in front of the massive rocks beside the pounding sea, had a ring of deep sincerity and purpose. It was very clear that the girl beside him was in love with him.

Tildy shut out of her mind the rise and fall of their conversation as they talked it over. Stephen, beside her, was pleased.

"These are great, Vera," he said with warmth. "Run that last segment again," he told the technician.

What about me, Tildy wailed silently in her mind. *I climbed over the jagged rocks for you. I walked on the*

122

cold wet sand. I stood barefoot while the edge of the icy sea slithered around my ankles and the spray drenched my face.

"Where will we be tomorrow?" Tildy asked at the first lull in their discussion. She had to get his attention.

Vera answered her, absently. "Clear back down to Los Angeles, Tildy. Steve has twelve appearances there, plus several meetings. We'll be there eight days—a long trip."

"Why so long?" she couldn't help asking.

Stephen answered her. "It's the largest city in the state, Tildy. About three million people. Does that answer your question?" His voice was dry. He might have been speaking to a small child.

Tildy felt as insignificant as a grain of sand upon the beach.

CHAPTER 13

In some place Tildy picked up a small pocket calendar. Election Day was always the first Tuesday in November. She marked that date and then began working toward it, marking off a day at a time. It was a little private game she played. She had not yet decided whether the marked off days referred to when she would be free of the campaign, or when she would lose Stephen.

By the time they made their third swing through Los Angeles, the campaign was intensified. Everyone was feeling the pressure and tempers often ran a little short.

No one ever had the courage to complain directly to Stephen, of course, but now and then one or the other would cast eyes heavenward in dismay at some request which would entail several hours of effort.

Oddly enough, it was Vera who actually lost her temper one night.

They had been driving back to their hotel from the fourth appearance of the day and all were nearly exhausted. Tildy lay back against the seat, her eyes half-closed, watching the brilliant neon signs of Ventura Boulevard flash by. Their last appearance had been in Sherman Oaks.

"Los Angeles means the angels, doesn't it?" she asked of no one in particular.

Stephen answered, moving slightly next to her. "Yes,

the actual name was *La Erección de un Pueblo con el Título de Reina de Los Angeles sobre el Río de la Porciuncula.* It means something like the founding of the town of the name of the Queen of the Angeles on the Porciuncula River."

The Spanish part of his reply had been in such quick and rhythmic Spanish that Tildy was surprised.

"Do you speak Spanish?" she asked.

"Yes," he said idly. "We have a vacation place in Acapulco where we go sometimes."

Suddenly frosty, calm, deliberate Vera went to pieces. She stiffened in her seat next to the other window. "What do you mean you speak Spanish!" she lashed out at him. "You never told me you spoke Spanish! Why didn't you tell me you spoke Spanish!" She was suddenly so furious she was shaking. Everybody in the car was stunned and for a moment there was total silence.

"It didn't occur to me," Stephen said evenly. He started to add something else and then fell silent, an odd look on his face. "I see what you mean," he said.

Alan, in the front seat, murmured softly, "Oh, good Lord."

Then Jeremy said, rather tentatively, "I suppose it's really too late now to do anything about scheduling any Spanish speeches for the Latino groups, isn't it? Or is it?"

"I don't know," Vera said tightly. "As soon as we get to the hotel, I'll get on the phone to Marv. If I had only known! You could pick up thousands of Mexican-American votes."

A wave of disbelief, then a terrible flooding of delight, washed over Tildy. Stephen had made a mistake! And such a stupid mistake! Every politician who had any sense wooed the ethnics, as they were called. They counted for huge blocks of votes in the given areas in which they had settled in great numbers. California had a large population of Mexican-Americans.

"I also have good Italian from a few summers in Italy," Stephen said. "Where might that help besides San Francisco?"

Something clicked in the back of Tildy's mind. She was

suddenly remembering her first meeting with Stephen Talbot, the moment when he had reluctantly handed her the papers entitled Candidate Profile. Instantly she came to his defense. He had not made the mistake, after all.

"All of that was in his Candidate Profile," she said. "He listed Spanish and Italian as fluent and French as passable," Tildy said.

Vera turned in her seat and stared at Tildy, her eyes brilliant with fury. "You're mistaken!" she said sharply.

"I guess we are all just awfully tired," Tildy answered smoothly. "When you call Marv tonight, why don't you ask him to look at his copy of the Profile, just to check it out."

"That's my girl," Stephen said, laughter in his voice. He was pleased that she had defended him and his hand clasped hers, twining his fingers between hers. Common sense told her it was just a friendly gesture, but suddenly her heart was singing.

"I grant you it's a bad mistake," he was saying, "whoever made it. All we can do now is try to correct it to the best of our abilities."

But Vera was deeply shaken, and Tildy felt almost sorry that she had remembered the Profile data. It was a serious error, however, and the agency was at fault in that Vera, Marv, or someone should have made use of Stephen's linguistic ability.

In order to make up for the blunder, they arranged a number of speaking dates for Mexican-American groups and worked them into the already crowded schedule. Stephen made speeches in fluent Spanish to many groups and Tildy was presented with a number of gifts from the responsive Latinos, because she would be the *novia* of the Spanish-speaking candidate for the United States Senate. Stephen told her that *novia* meant bride. She had a *piñata* for use next Christmas if she wanted to, two *mantillas* of very good lace, several items of hand-worked leather, three brightly embroidered Mexican blouses, four fans, and one sombrero with a brim wider than her umbrella.

Tildy enjoyed the Latino gatherings because there was usually music and food. She enjoyed the happy mariachi and the sad guitars—they never seemed to play anything happy on the guitars.

Stephen gained four more points in popularity, according to the California polls, and the undecideds took an upward turn. This was looked upon as a very good sign, because it took points away from the two big parties.

Twice they went back to Sacramento for a few days' respite from the campaign. One evening Bruce called and asked if she would go some place with him for dinner. They went to a small steak-and-lobster house and, within the walls of the leather-upholstered booth, Bruce talked enthusiastically of his work in the campaign and wanted to hear about her experiences on the road with Stephen. She learned that he was traveling almost as much as they were, up and down the state, working with youth groups, eliciting aid for his brother, and rallying the youth vote in his behalf. Despite the fact that all their conversation was about the campaign, it was an enjoyable evening. Bruce's obvious devotion to his brother made Tildy a little sad for him.

"You know, he could lose," Tildy said tentatively at one point.

"Never! He can't possibly lose! It's going just great, Tildy."

Another time, toward the end of September, he took her sight-seeing, deploring the fact that she knew so little about Sacramento, the state capital. It was a very enjoyable day. They had fun and laughed a lot.

"You know, Tildy," Bruce said when he left her at her apartment, "I'll be kind of sorry when it's all over. I don't suppose we'll ever see you again, will we?"

It was the first time he had referred outright to the engagement being false.

"I—doubt it," she smiled. "But who knows, maybe our paths will cross again." But she felt sure it would not happen. Back in her apartment, she crossed off another day from her small calendar.

They appeared at the Los Angeles County Fair held at the Pomona Fair Grounds. It was unbearably hot and Tildy longed for San Francisco as she sat on the platform, trying to look cool and composed in her pale green cotton dress and her white off-the-face straw hat. She resolved never to wear a choker necklace again in this kind of weather. But despite the heat, Stephen held his audience and they applauded him enthusiastically several times during his speech. For the last few minutes of the speech, Tildy had thought longingly of the swimming pool back at the motel. She could hardly wait to dive into it, slicing the cool water cleanly. Automatically, she stood up with the others when the speech was finished and applauded. Then, waiting desperately to leave. to escape, she heard Stephen accept an invitation to accompany a group through the livestock exhibits.

"You'd like that, wouldn't you, Tildy?"

Marveling at herself, she gave the man a brilliant smile. "I'd love it," she said. "As a city girl, I don't often get a chance to see any animals but small household pets. I did see the buffalo in Golden Gate Park last year, and each year they have a Christmas pageant with live sheep, and of course Stephen has horses, because he rides." She wondered where she had picked up that last bit of information.

She was learning to be a political woman. Somehow or other, no matter what happened, or to whom she was talking, she had picked up the knack of quickly turning the attention of the group back to the candidate. Stephen had said she was a good campaigner. She was beginning to believe it.

There was a crowd in the livestock tents and Tildy found herself next to a tiny, white-haired little woman with brilliant blue eyes and a delighted interest in her surroundings.

"You know," she confided to Tildy, "I just love Mr. Talbot. I do so hope he wins!"

"Oh, I do, too," Tildy agreed, sliding into her routine of generalities. "He has such a wonderful grasp of the issues."

"I—I wanted to help, if I could," the little woman said, glancing over her shoulder. "You see," she seemed embarrassed, "Rod, that's my husband, Rod—I hate to say this, but Rod isn't going to vote for Mr. Talbot. First time we haven't voted the same in thirty-seven years."

"Well, perhaps you can convince him," Tildy smiled.

"Not when Rod makes up his mind," the woman sighed. "I do want to contribute something to his campaign, though," she said timidly. "It would be from me personally. Could you help me?"

"I can give you the address where you can mail it," Tildy offered. "It's certainly most kind of you." Somehow she had got separated from the rest of her group and wanted to get back in case any pictures were taken. Stephen had told her more than once to stay in camera range.

"That's just it, I can't." The woman seemed genuinely distressed. "I—I have a little money of my own—that Rod doesn't know about. Could I just give it to you?"

"I?" Tildy asked. No one had ever quite made that suggestion before. "I—suppose so."

Instantly the woman had opened her black plastic purse and extracted a tightly folded bit of blue paper.

"I was so hoping I could speak to you," she said in an earnest whisper. "I already made out the check and a little receipt. I knew you would be terribly pressed for time. Could you just put this money into the campaign—for anything at all—and sign this receipt for me? Political contributions are deductible, you know. I do wish the government wasn't so sticky about getting receipts. Maybe Mr. Talbot can do something about the income tax people when he gets to Washington. Here, take the check, dear."

Tildy read the receipt quickly. It seemed a simple, clear receipt for a political contribution. She signed it hurriedly. Then she unfolded the check. It was for one hundred dollars made out to Tildy Marshall.

"But this is made out to me," Tildy said in confusion.

"Of course, dear. Just you use the money for something in the campaign. I don't want my name to show. Rod, you know, mightn't like it. He'd known if I got a thank-you card or something." Suddenly in the push of the crowd the little woman melted away. Tildy thrust the check into her handbag and hurriedly rejoined Stephen, who was looking around for her.

They returned to Sacramento Tuesday evening with plans to be on the road again Thursday morning.

One whole day of rest!

Tildy wanted simply to drop into bed, but minute by minute she made herself go through the routine of cleaning and creaming her face. Her skin must be flawless before the relentless cameras. She thanked heaven that she could wait until tomorrow to do her nails. One whole free day. Never had she realized how precious idle time could be. And no alarm clock tomorrow. One lovely day when she would not have to claw her way foggily out of deep sleep to the jangle of the alarm clock or telephone bell.

But the telephone did ring, again and again, shrilling away, as her mind, deep in sleep for hours, struggled against hearing it. Finally, she stumbled out of bed, trailing the covers on the floor, and fumbled in the darkness to get to the living room phone.

"Hello! Hello! It's me, Dottie. Is that you, Tildy?"

"Yes," Tildy said, seeming almost drugged with sleep. "Who is it? Dottie?"

"Yes, Dottie. You know, from down at campaign headquarters."

"Yes, yes, of course. Dottie," she mumbled. "Wait. Can you wait a moment?" She put the receiver down and stumbled into the bathroom, hitting her shoulder a sharp crack on the doorway. She dashed cold water onto her face.

"Sorry, Dottie," she said when she got back to the telephone. "I just couldn't seem to wake up. What time is it?" It wasn't yet morning, because the room had been still in total blackness, with just the faint moonglow from outside.

"I don't know. I can't see my watch. Tildy, you have to help me."

"Of course. Now, calm down, Dottie." Tildy said with much more assurance than she felt. A sickish apprehension was beginning to pervade her mind. She reached over and snapped on the small desk lamp. The clock beneath said it was three o'clock.

"I have to see you. I have to see somebody," Dottie was saying. "I drove all the way to San Francisco and back after work and I've been looking all over. I can't find Lennie!"

"Lennie Bishop? Did you call his number?"

"Of course I called his number! It doesn't answer. I—Tildy, I can't get in touch with him. I want to talk to you."

"All right. Of course." Tildy could hear the smooth, pleasant political-wife sound of her voice. Dottie was a campaign worker and she was wildly upset about something, Tildy had to smooth it over before it created a problem for the campaign.

"I don't mean on the telephone. I'm down at headquarters. Can you come? You have to!"

"Of course, of course. Please, Dottie, just calm down. I'll get dressed and be there as quickly as I can." As she hung up the receiver, she was appalled at herself. It was 3:00 A.M. and she had no business dashing about the city at that time in the morning. The whole thing was ridiculous! Even as she fumed about it, she hurried into the bathroom and somehow within minutes she was dressed in jeans, T-shirt, and sneakers and tying up her hair in a scarf. Snatching up a sweater and her keys, she rushed out the door.

There was plenty of street parking at this time of the morning and she drove up in front of the headquarters. It was dark. Dottie must have gone. Then she saw Dottie just inside the door. Wise girl. She had turned off the lights so it would not be obvious to any idle passerby that there was one lone woman in the building. Street crime was one of the things Stephen wanted to do something about.

"Oh, thank you, Tildy! I thought you'd never get here. I'm so worried and I tried and tried to find Lennie, and I couldn't and—I'm so tired," she finished desperately, sounding like an exhausted child. Tildy's heart went out to her. She reached over and pushed back the girl's tousled brown hair.

"What is it, Dottie? What's the matter? How can I help?"

They went inside and shut the door. "Well," Dottie said tiredly, "I guess I'd better start at the beginning. I'm not working for Marv. I'm working for Lennie."

Tildy looked at her blankly.

"Lennie has worked in other campaigns, for other candidates he was backing. Then, when he and the others persuaded Steve to run for the Senate, he sort of—looks after things. He's very wise about politics."

"I—don't know what you mean."

"He said that when the campaign got going well, someone might try to do something to hurt Steve."

"Hurt him?" Tildy felt suddenly cold.

"Damage his campaign, I mean. He was right, they did. I'm supposed to watch out for things that—don't seem right and then report them to Lennie. He checks things out then. You see?"

Tildy was beginning to.

"That was why I once saw you meeting him in San Francisco," she murmured.

"Did you? He tried to be careful, choose unlikely places. He doesn't like to talk about things on the phone. Anyhow, trouble has started. Did you know about the false information that is being filtered to Vera to use in the speeches?"

"Yes, I know," Tildy said quietly, remembering the anguish of being suspected herself.

"Well, I found out who is doing it, only where is Lennie when I need him? All I'm supposed to do is pass along the word to Lennie. I can't mess around with campaign stuff. That's why I called you. You're Steve's fiancée. You could call him—get him here—something."

"What campaign stuff?" Tildy asked, her voice sounding firm regardless of an inward shivering.

"The stuff in Marv's desk."

"In Marv's desk!" Tildy gasped.

"Yes. It's Marv. Marv is doing it."

133

"Oh no! Not Marv." Tildy was stunned. Kindly, genial, helpful Marv. It just couldn't be! Anybody but Marv.

"It is. It is, Tildy. Come and let me show you."

Woodenly Tildy followed the agitated Dottie back to Marv's office.

"In here. In this drawer," Dottie was saying frantically. She was almost crying. She opened one of the deep file drawers of the desk and pulled out a folder of campaign information, taking out a single sheet and handing it to Tildy. Hating it, Tildy made herself look at it. It appeared to be a sheet of data about one of the opponents, all neatly typed up from the researcher.

"Now, look at this, Tildy." Dottie handed her another sheet, much folded, which she had been gripping in her hand. "This is the original sheet from the researcher."

It looked like the same information, but with several changes written over it in Marv's bold handwriting.

"Where did you get this?" Tildy asked, her hands unsteady.

"Behind the paper shredder. I guess he was destroying some papers and this one slid behind the machine and he didn't notice. As soon as I found it, I started looking for a retyped version. I knew if it was in the data folder that Vera would use it. He changed it, Tildy. Now Vera will get the wrong information again."

Oh, not Marv. Tildy wanted to cry. Betrayal was one thing, but betrayal by a friend was such a bitter, hurtful thing. She liked him so. They all did, depended on him, regarded him as one of the mainstays of the campaign.

"What am I going to do, Tildy? I've got to get this to Lennie so he can handle it."

"Lennie is out of town," Tildy heard herself saying remotely. "When you called, I was so sleepy I had forgotten it. You can't reach him."

"What can I do?" Dottie whispered, her eyes huge.

"I'll take care of it," Tildy said calmly, folding the sheets up and putting them into her jeans pocket.

Dottie clutched at her a moment. "Tildy. Thank you. How can you be so calm! I see you sometimes—you know,

134

on the TV news—always so smiling and serene, never getting upset. Oh, Tildy," Dottie was close to tears. "You're just like a princess."

"Yes, the well-known Serene Highness. All princesses run around town at three in the morning wearing jeans. Come on, Dottie, we'll go back to my place," she said briskly. Oh, Marv, how could you do this to Stephen? She felt a kind of inward crying.

Driving Dottie back across town, Tildy said, "Have you had any sleep at all tonight?"

"No," Dottie said wearily. "I worked late and then I started my hunting around the office, and then I spent hours trying to find Lennie." She sounded exhausted and sad, which Tildy understood completely. She wondered how Stephen would feel, and she felt her hands gripping the steering wheel. This would hurt Stephen. She would see it in his eyes, hear it in his voice, feel it herself, because she loved him so.

"Have you had anything to eat?" she asked Dottie as she unlocked her apartment door.

"No," Dottie said dolefully. "There wasn't time."

Kindly, competently, Tildy heated some milk and a sweet roll she had picked up for her own breakfast.

"This will hold you until morning," she said, bringing it to Dottie, who sat dejectedly in the living room. "Then tomorrow I'll take you out to breakfast. I'll treat you to hotcakes and sausage—anything you want."

Dottie looked up, her eyes shining with unshed tears. "What are you going to do with that?" she asked, indicating the papers in Tildy's pocket.

"I'm going to give it to Stephen," she said, and then realized that she was going to do exactly that, and as soon as possible. She had an instinctive conviction that she should not wait. If it concerned Stephen's campaign, Stephen would want to know now.

While Dottie was eating her roll and sipping her hot milk, Tildy dialed Stephen's phone number. It rang at the other end three times. He was as tired as everyone else. But when he did answer, his voice sounded wide awake.

135

Tildy chose her words carefully, having been told to always be careful on the telephone for fear of electronic surveillance.

"Stephen, something has come up about the campaign that I think you will want to discuss. Could you come over?"

There was a moment of silence. He didn't question or demur. He wasn't appalled that she woke him at four in the morning. He said simply, "Certainly, I'll be right there."

Twenty minutes later he was in the apartment with them, looking very unlike the candidate for the United States Senate, in faded jeans and a cream turtleneck sweater, his hair windblown. He saw Dottie instantly and greeted her with a smile, then, because Dottie was there, he kissed Tildy lightly.

"Now what difficulty have you girls got into?" he asked pleasantly.

Dottie, awestruck at this informal rendezvous with the candidate seemed to have lost her voice.

"Did you know that Dottie was working for Lennie?" Tildy asked him.

"Not specifically. Lennie told me once that he had some people planted in the organization who were keeping their eyes open. Are you one of them, Dottie?" He turned his pleasant gaze to her, but Tildy heard the even tone of his voice.

"Yes," Dottie said. She glanced at Tildy imploringly.

Tildy took the papers from her pocket. She had to hurt him. She, Tildy, had to tell him about Marv. She passed her tongue over her suddenly dry lips.

"Dottie came upon something which seems to show—who is falsifying Vera's data."

"Who is it?" His voice was calm, toneless. She had the odd feeling that he had been in situations like this before. He was preparing himself. She felt it. It was in the taut line of his jaw, the steely quality in his eyes. He was a fighter preparing to take a blow he couldn't avoid.

Wordlessly, she handed him the two sheets of paper. She wanted to clasp his strong hands, stroke his face, push back his tousled hair—anything to distract him, to ease

136

the tension. He glanced swiftly at one paper and then the other. He knew instantly what it was, and he knew Marv's handwriting. He said softly, "Oh, no, not Marv." Then he turned away from them and walked almost aimlessly across the room.

Tildy, having seen the naked hurt in his eyes for a moment, couldn't speak at all.

"Do you happen to know why, Dottie?" he asked, not turning around.

"No," she said. Then, "I—I'm sorry." She was twisting her grubby hands together.

He turned. "No need to be sorry," he said gently. "You've done your share, certainly. You tried to reach Lennie and couldn't, I guess."

"Yes."

"What—will you do now?" Tildy found her voice at last.

"I'll see Marv as soon as I can. Tomorrow morning. This morning, actually. It's after four. Thank you, Dottie." He came over to the couch where she was still sitting and bent over to kiss the top of her head. Color flamed into the girl's face and she was speechless.

"And thank you, Tildy, for getting to me so fast." He held out his hand and she took it. He wanted her to come with him into the hallway.

Outside in the hallway she couldn't help asking, "Why! Why did Marv do it!"

"Money," Stephen said, his voice a little dull. "People will do a lot for money. I'll get rid of him, certainly. He is no more use to the campaign. But I'll have to talk to him first."

"You could just call the agency and fire him," Tildy said. She hated the idea of Stephen enduring a confrontation with a man he had liked so much and who had betrayed him.

"I could. That would get rid of him. It would also finish him in the publicity business. I think I may want to handle it differently. I don't know yet."

"When will you know?"

"When I find out why he needed the money. I—" he sounded oddly apologetic. "I have to be careful in judgments of people in matters of money. Everyone knows that I've always been honest in my dealings. It's easy for me. I never needed to be dishonest. That's why I have to be careful. Thanks for handling this, Tildy. You really are becoming a terrific campaigner. When you fall in love and marry, I hope you marry some guy who is running for office—but not against me."

Tildy clasped suddenly unsteady hands behind her. She watched him go toward the elevator. He wasn't standing so straight now. The defection of Marv had hit him hard. At the elevator he turned and came back, taking out his billfold. He extracted a large bill and handed it to Tildy.

"When you go out tomorrow, buy Dottie a nice gift. You will know what she likes. Good night."

Tildy stood in the hall after he had gone, tears brimming over. How like him. How very like him. Never making any mistakes, never forgetting anything. Hurt as he was, he would think about a gift for Dottie because she had done him a favor. Oh, Stephen . . .

CHAPTER 14

In October they rode in an open car in the Columbus Day Parade in San Francisco, and Stephen made a speech which included several fluent Italian phrases, partly in the Sicilian dialect. He was very well received.

San Francisco always made a big celebration of Columbus Day, with local Italian-Americans donning the costumes of Columbus's time and performing an amateur pageant of the old story. This year Queen Isabella was quite pretty but Columbus had difficulty rising from his knees. Tildy smiled and applauded along with all the rest, thinking all the while of Marv. She would never know what had occurred between the two men, but Marv had suddenly been called away from his work in the campaign. A plausible reason was given that he had to be transferred to the agency's New York office. That this might be unusual in the middle of a campaign few people took note of. Since she had helped in the exposure, Stephen did her the courtesy of talking to her briefly about it.

"I had a long talk with Marv," he said, his gaze fixed on something outside the window of the hotel they were in. If the hurt still pained him, he was hiding it.

"Why did he do it?" Tildy had to ask.

"I'm sorry, Tildy. I—can't go into that, much as I appreciate your help in the matter. Marv told me things I don't think he has ever told anybody else. I can't betray his confidence. Just leave it that he had urgent personal reasons."

"He betrayed your confidence," Tildy couldn't help saying.

Stephen waited a moment before he replied, then he spoke slowly. "Yes, and I got rid of him, but I can't pass judgment because I've never been tested like that. The most I could do in conscience was get him out of my life, protect my campaign. Beyond that, it's not my place to mete out any punishment or take any revenge."

Afterward Tildy wondered, but didn't ask, what he would have done if she had been the defector in the group. She clung to the idea that he would have been as merciful, would have taken into consideration the reason why.

Meanwhile, a Mr. Wade McKinley took over Marv's duties and she wondered if she would ever see Marv again. Stephen had said in the beginning that politics was full of strange pitfalls. Apparently having to write off a trusted employee was one of them.

The incident was effectively buried in the increased work and excitement of the campaign itself. Knowledgeable people commented now that the campaign was beginning to peak. The billboards contracted for earlier began to appear on streets, highways, atop buildings, and in vacant lots. The gap seemed to be closing between Stephen and his Democrat and Republican opponents—there seemed no obvious winner among the three now. Everything depended upon the growing group who called themselves undecided. The news media was creating excitement by its continued stress on how close the race was going to be.

During the brief respites in Sacramento, there was almost no rest, for Tildy was included in Stephen's personal social life more. Everything he said or did now appeared in the papers or on the evening news on television, and it benefited them to create opportunities for the news media. They never knew until they got back to Sacramento just what the evening held in store. Jean, Stephen's sister, took care of this part of it.

The accepted invitations were always selected with care.

140

There were no intimate little dinners with Stephen's friends in their homes. Instead, they went with them to the opera, both in San Francisco and in Sacramento, to a couple of symphonies, to outstanding restaurants, and a few plays—but always in public, where chance of news coverage was best.

Tildy was uneasy with Stephen's friends, who were a young married group, with few single people among them. It seemed that Stephen was almost the last of them to marry. The talk among the women was of homes, children, husbands' careers. Tildy joined in because she had to; it was part of the job. It grated especially on her nerves because it came so close to out-and-out lying. She began to develop small catch-phrases in order to avoid this.

Someone always asked about Stephen's future political plans. If he did win this Senate seat, did he plan to try and go higher? She would fling out her hands in a graceful gesture.

"Who knows what Stephen is going to do tomorrow? I can just keep up with what he did yesterday and today," she would say, and they would always laugh, thinking they had been answered.

Frequently women asked about the wedding plans and Tildy could reply with fragments of truth. Yes, she had always planned to have a church wedding. Yes, she would wear white; in fact, she planned to wear her mother's wedding gown. No, she had no idea where she would go on her honeymoon—she wanted to be surprised. All these little comments were true, and someday they might happen, but not with Stephen Talbot, and this she kept hidden from his friends. It cost her dearly.

At a dinner one evening someone asked, "Do you and Stephen plan to have a big family?" Suddenly there it was. For a moment she was caught short, her glibness deserting her. The questioner was the wife of one of Stephen's law school friends, and she herself was pregnant and delighted about it. There was a kind of serenity in her face and all her thoughts touched on the coming infant. This was a blessing, because she failed to notice that Tildy faltered and seemed for a moment distracted.

141

"Stephen and I have never discussed children," she said finally. She held her breath a moment, but the woman did not pursue the matter beyond asking, "Do you want a family?"

To this Tildy could answer instantly, "Yes," not realizing how fervent it sounded. She had a brief mental image of herself, Stephen, and their children, then she escaped to the ladies room and sat down at one of the dressing tables and looked at herself.

Yes, she wanted that more than anything else in the world but it would never happen. For a moment she was utterly tired, depleted, exhausted. She thought she might put her head down on the vanity—just for a moment— and try to forget about Stephen and the life she would never have.

But this she was not allowed either. Another of his friends popped into the room.

"Oh, here you are, Tildy. Stephen was asking where you had done to."

"I'm coming right now," Tildy said. "I just wanted to check my makeup."

That evening, as Stephen was driving her back to her apartment, she felt her control slipping. The buildup of pressure, strain, and physical fatigue suddenly came together and she knew with dawning horror that she was going to cry. She had the feeling that this irritated Stephen more than anything else she did. It started with an incredible aching in her throat. She tried to put everything out of her mind. She tried counting street lights. Desperately she turned her face to the window, away from him, and tried to control her breathing while the tears started down her cheeks. Finally she had to grope in her handbag.

"Reach into my side pocket," Stephen said remotely. "You'll find a spare handkerchief."

He knew.

Then it didn't matter and the sobbing burst forth. She huddled over in the seat and in a moment he took one hand from the steering wheel and thrust the handkerchief into her hand. She had not wept like this since her parents' death. She felt hopeless, helpless, because she had found her love and lost it. She would love this man until she died, and she couldn't have him.

"What's the matter, Tildy? Can you talk now?" he asked when the crying subsided into an occasional shuddering sob.

"I'm just tired," she said, her voice barely audible. "I want to go home."

"I'm taking you home. But I have to observe the posted speed limit. I had two drinks before dinner and a brandy afterward. If I get cited for speeding the press will imply drunk driving."

"I don't mean to the apartment, I mean home to San Francisco. I want to see Uncle James." The desperation came through in her tone. She knew with great clarity that she needed to see him, to talk to him, to heal her soul in her uncle's gentle wisdom and humor. For just a little while she had to be free of the suffocation of being a political person, free of the relentless glare of the limelight and—maybe—free from this longing for Stephen.

She would curl up on the window seat in the living room of the old shabby flat that fronted on Golden Gate Park. Just she and Uncle James would be there. They would talk together from time to time, with great stretches of comfortable silence between, just like old times, before any of this had happened.

"I have to go home," she said intensely. "Just—for a day. Just for half a day."

"I'm sorry, Tildy, but we have to fly to Palm Springs tomorrow morning." It was said kindly but beneath the kindness was the ruthlessness, the implacable forging onward toward the goal.

Tildy lay back against the seat limply. It was no use. He had asked her what was the matter and she had evaded by saying that she was tired. What would he have said if she had replied with the whole truth? *I love you, Stephen. I'm sick with love for you, and because of this I must escape from you for a while.* What would he say? He would be stunned. Appalled. Embarrassed.

Pondering this idea, she watched the night scenes move by, dully and without interest.

"Where are we going?" she asked after a while. "This isn't the way to the apartment."

"You seem so—desperate, I thought I'd drive you over to San Francisco. It's an outrageous hour, but you said your uncle is addicted to the late show. Maybe he'll still be up."

"No!" she said tautly. Uncle James's flat was the haven, the hiding place. She didn't know why, but she wildly rejected the idea of Stephen taking her there now— Stephen waiting with grim patience during a stilted visit with Uncle James, Stephen glancing around the shabby flat, not missing any detail, and perhaps mentally criticizing Uncle James because he had so little. "No! I don't want you to take me there. I don't want—I want—"

"All right. I get the message. What you really want is to be rid of the campaign. Rid of me. I understand that, but we have an agreement. Do you want out of it?"

Blunt, merciless, the words came, his voice cold.

There was no way in the world she could ever explain to him. She leaned against the back of the seat. "Just take me back to my apartment," she said.

"As you wish," he answered grimly, easing the powerful car over into the left lane for the next turnoff from the Freeway. The rest of the drive was made in thick silence.

At the doorway of her apartment, he unlocked it and dropped the key back onto her palm.

"I'll say one thing before I go." His voice was remote and utterly cold. "I know you disdain everything I am doing. I'm sorry about that, but we have less than a month to go. The first week in November you will collect your bonus and be free of it all, free of me. Can you stick it out that much longer?"

How could she answer him? What could she say? The last thing he wanted to hear was the truth—that she had fallen in love with him, gotten emotionally involved, as he had warned against. Carefully she said the only thing she could say.

"I'm sorry I got hysterical. Of course, I want to stay with the campaign to the finish. Please just forget my antics tonight."

"All right." He tried to smile, but the strain was showing even with him. "Go mark another day off your damn little calendar. We've got a whole new set of problems to face tomorrow. But the first Wednesday in November you are free because the election will be over."

She felt her face flaming. He had noticed the calendar at some time. He had guessed what it was for. He turned and, without another word, walked toward the elevator. Tildy escaped into her apartment.

All the next day, during the Palm Springs appearances, she watched him covertly. No matter how he felt, his performance was flawless. She had a deep sense of admiration for him, and she tried to make her performance just as flawless.

There were appearances scheduled the next day for nearby towns, so they stayed in the Palm Springs hotel for the night. There was suddenly a whole vacant evening ahead of them. It seemed unbelievable, an idea to be approached with caution, tantalizing one with anticipation.

"What we ought to do tonight is settle down and make some hard plans for the victory balls in the five key cities," an aide suggested.

"Are you so sure he's going to win?" Tildy asked.

"No, Tildy," Vera answered, her crispness returning. "But all candidates have victory balls in every possible place. They are scheduled and planned for in advance. It's a terrible expense, but it's all part of the political tradition."

"What happens if the candidate loses?" Tildy couldn't help asking.

Alan answered, moaning, "Tildy, don't even speak of it! I've been to two losing ones. It's ghastly. Everybody tries to be happy and laugh it up. And every other minute you discover someone in tears because the candidate lost, after all that work and trying. The men get sadder and drunker and sadder and drunker. Then the candidate

145

comes with his family looking like death warmed over—and makes his speech."

"Speech?"

"You bet. He has to concede, admit he's licked. He has to congratulate his opponent, thank his workers, and plead with the voters who voted for him to stick together as Americans first, party adherence notwithstanding. He has to be gracious, and a good fellow, and it's tearing his guts out. It's awful."

"But if he wins?"

"Now you've got it!" Alan sprang up from his chair. "The old victory spirit! Then the thing is a blast. Everybody is in heaven and it doesn't break up until daylight. It's a riot, a gas. It's—" He would have gone on but the telephone rang.

Stephen, who was seated closest to it, reached over and picked up the receiver. As he answered, he was half-laughing. The younger man's high spirits had eased the tension.

They fell silent and listened to his side of the conversation. He didn't say much, with long pauses for listening in between. They knew that the man calling was McKinley, Marv's replacement in the Sacramento office. Stephen tried to reassure him, but without much conviction. He said, "All right, I appreciate your telling me. When Lennie gets through with this audit, have him call me." Then, "That's all right. It doesn't matter what time it is." Then he replaced the receiver and there was an odd little silence.

"What is it?" Vera, intent as a lynx, bent over his chair. She looked as if she wanted to touch him.

"McKinley knows some of the people in one of the other campaigns," Stephen said quietly. "He got wind of a rumor that we are in for some legal trouble with the government over some unreported contributions."

"No way!" Jeremy said, astounded, from the far side of the room. "Lennie Bishop would never let that happen! He's really on top of everything. I know him. I worked for him in other campaigns."

"Well," Stephen said dryly, "there seems to have been

a slipup. The opposition has the word out that we aren't reporting all individual contributions. They say they have actual proof of one unreported hundred-dollar contribution. That's all it takes—proof of one. Then it will be assumed that we've skimmed off thousand of dollars."

"You said proof?" Jeremy's eyes had narrowed. "What kind of proof?"

"It's hard for our people to pin down. But they say they think there is an existing receipt for a one-hundred-dollar contribution for which there will be no corresponding entry in our deposits or reports to the government. It's bound to be a simple clerical mistake. They're sure to find it."

"They won't find it," Tildy said, her voice sounding faint. She had trouble speaking and her mouth had gone dry. Her hands, though not shaking, felt icy cold.

Everyone looked over at her. Nobody spoke for a moment. Then Stephen said, "Tildy?" rather tentatively. "You're white as a ghost—what is it? What's the matter?" He was out of his chair and standing beside her.

"I—have it," she said, trying to speak clearly. There seemed to be a gathering of grayness in the corners of the room. That grayness had happened once before, the one time in her life when she had fainted.

"You what?"

"I have the hundred dollars. A woman gave it to me. She had a receipt all ready. I was supposed to put the money into the campaign. I just haven't done it yet."

Vera hissed softly, "You little idiot!"

Alan moaned. "It was a trap, Tildy—how could you!"

And Jeremy said sickly, "They were setting Steve up."

From somewhere Tildy found the strength to reach down to her handbag on the floor beside her chair. She felt a dim sense of grief at the duplicity of that sweet, white-haired old lady. She kept her eyes averted from Stephen, after a glimpse of his face, set, hard. She had to establish her innocence, if nothing else. She could not let him harbor the idea that she too had defected the way Marv had. She would have to—some way—spare him that.

147

Not really believing that she could be so poised under pressure, Tildy opened the handbag, took out her billfold, and extracted the check, handing it to him.

Stephen took it. Vera was leaning over his shoulder with both Alan and Jeremy now, all able to get a good look at it.

"It's made out to you," Vera said grimly. "Are you taking a leaf out of Marv's book?"

"She hasn't cashed it," Alan offered hopefully, his expressive eyes clouded with worry.

Stephen was looking at the check, his mouth grim.

"What good will that do?" Jeremy asked. "She took it and gave a receipt, I guess. Did you give a receipt, Tildy?"

"Yes, she had it all made out." She was astonished how calm she sounded. She wondered about it remotely. Was this the way Stephen had learned, meeting and facing down countless challenges of his life? Maybe this hectic last few months had taught her something, matured her in some way she had not been aware of. She had a fragmentary memory of little Dottie, so harassed the night in campaign headquarters. *I see you sometimes—on the TV news—always so smiling and serene.* Dottie was another one she wasn't going to let down. She couldn't manage the smile, but she did manage an outward serenity.

Finally Stephen spoke. "Tell me how it happened, Tildy."

"It was at that fair in Pomona in the livestock exhibits. A woman—a pleasant, little, white-haired woman—approached me. She said she wanted to make a secret contribution to the campaign. She was supporting you, her husband was not. She said she wanted me to filter it into the campaign so her name wouldn't appear. She didn't want to get a thank-you card. I took the check and put it in my billfold. I intended to give it to Lennie, but we've been so tightly scheduled that I just haven't had the chance. I should have dropped it in the mail to him, I—wanted to ask him to be sure she didn't get any thank-you card." She felt incredibly stupid.

Alan said thoughtfully, "Maybe she wanted you to cash it first and contribute anonymous cash."

148

"No," Stephen said, still looking at the check in his hand. "She made it out to Tildy to tempt Tildy to cash it and use it for herself, not give it to the campaign. Then there would be no connection." His voice sounded faintly sad. "I'm sure she would rather have given Tildy cash but was afraid, I guess, that Tildy might suspect the trap."

"Yes," Vera said quickly. "You're right. The fact that she did give a check gives us a way out, doesn't it, Steve?"

"Yes," Stephen said calmly. "All we need do now is for Tildy to endorse the check over to the campaign and give it to Lennie. That way the contribution will appear correctly listed in our deposits and reports. And this woman's name will show, this Mattie Halbrand. She has rather a nice handwriting." A brief cynical twist touched his mouth. He handed the check to Tildy.

Tildy took the check and Jeremy handed her his pen. She wrote the endorsement carefully, exactly as Stephen dictated it. Then Stephen turned to Alan.

"I'm afraid you aren't going to spend the evening in the pool, Alan. I want you to go down to the airport and get this check up to Sacramento—fast. Lennie has worked his head off searching for this lousy hundred dollars."

Without a word Alan took the check and headed for the door, his evening plans forgotten.

"Well, one more problem solved," Stephen said, walking toward the door. "Are you coming, Tildy? I promised to take you to dinner." He had not, but she followed his lead. For some reason he wanted out, but he wanted her with him.

"Do you want to talk to me about the check?" she asked as they waited for the elevator.

"No, you explained it. I just wanted to get away from the others. Sometimes I just have to get free of it all—the campaign, the hassle."

"You?" she gasped, as the elevator stopped and they got in.

"Yes, me. Golden Boy Candidate." He laughed as he said it.

Later, over dinner, he continued in the same manner.

"I know what people think and say—rich guy playing at politics. Well, if I win, they'll get a surprise. But things have been building up for several weeks now. When that damned phony check came up, I thought for a minute—" He paused. "I thought someone had gotten to you. Right now I don't think I could take another Marv incident."

She looked at him silently, taking in every line of his face, and had a fleeting idea of the odd vulnerability of the very rich—never being absolutely sure of any other person because of the money. He had possibly never known the security of a bond such as that between herself and Uncle James, because neither had anything the other wanted beyond love and respect. Their regard was open and free, untinged by any question.

"You don't—have to do all this," she said tentatively. "Bruce said you had been working in your father's law firm."

"I was. It was a good life but sterile. I could do more. And besides, the campaign itself is the worst part. If I win, what I will win will be a six-year term in the Senate. My godfather was a Senator. I knew him well. We were good friends. I watched—sometimes I helped him sweat out the campaigns. But each time he won, he had before him that whole campaign-free six years to work in the Senate. He worked his head off. He was that kind of man, but it was all good. He was doing something worthwhile. The campaign, the hassle to get the office in the first place, is the only bad part of it. The intervening years are good—not necessarily happy, but good."

She listened to him, transfixed. He had never talked to her with this easy, open attitude. He was looking at her thoughtfully. "You know, in the beginning, when I went over your résumé, application, and the reports—there didn't seem to be any boyfriend in the picture."

"There wasn't—isn't. Just casual dates now and then."

"I was thinking that when you marry, you ought to pick somebody who needs a wife he can put on display."

"A politician?"

"Not necessarily, although you have turned into a major asset to any politician. No, I was thinking in terms of some man with the potential to be a top executive." He was smiling. "I see you as a sort of perfect wife for him."

It was a nice compliment, but he had shattered the magic. She lowered her eyes, concentrating on taking a sip of her coffee, and then another sip. *I love you,* her heart cried. *There won't be anyone else.*

CHAPTER 15

After they left the town of Calexico, on the Mexican border, they hurried back to Los Angeles, where Stephen had an appearance on a popular talk show. Then back down to San Diego again. Eventually they worked their way up the coast of California one more time.

The roughest day they had was when they made seven appearances. Tildy felt like a zombie and could think of nothing but getting back to the hotel to fall into her bed. In order to stay with it, and keep up her portrayal of the eager, young woman who was the candidate's fiancée, she had made herself little promises during the last two appearances. She would not wait to shower. She would not bother to cream her face. Bed, sleep, that was the wonderful prize waiting for her back at the hotel.

But when they finally got back, there was an urgent phone message from Stephen's father. The rest of them stood in the sitting room of the suite while Stephen called him back. Tildy thought vaguely that they were all pretty dedicated, since none of them ever left until Stephen told them to go. Now they waited. Alan stood by the window, his hands braced on the ledge, looking out but not really seeing anything. Jeremy was slouched in a chair trying to keep awake. Vera stood just inside the doorway, where she had stopped. Her face looked gaunt, and she was rubbing the back of her neck with both hands, head tilted back, eyes closed.

"I see," Stephen was saying. "All right, Father, if you think it's necessary." Slowly he hung up the receiver, and turned to look at them. His face was composed, but his eyes were haggard.

"Sir, are you all right?" Alan asked, turning from the window.

"Yes. Nothing is wrong that some sleep won't cure," Stephen said easily, then he paused as if reluctant to go on. "I have to get back to Sacramento tonight. I'd suggest that you all stay on, but we have to get out of there so early tomorrow morning that it might not be worth it. I'll give you a choice, though. Any of you who want to stay on here and get a few hours sleep, and then make it to Sacramento by eight tomorrow morning—that would be okay. I could send the plane back down to Fresno for you. It's not all that far."

They all demurred, pretending not to be exhausted. It was no problem. They would all be glad to go back to Sacramento now. They would sleep when they got there.

They all dozed on the short flight from Fresno to Sacramento but, at least to Tildy, it brought small relief from the sheer bone tiredness she felt.

"Would you three mind taking a cab?" Stephen asked the others, disembarking from the plane. "My Jag should be here and I'll drop Tildy off."

Through her fatigue-laden senses, Tildy was worried about him, why he had had suddenly to come back, why his father had summoned him. No one in his family had ever disturbed him before when he was on tour.

"Tildy, do you mind if we stop at the house first?" he asked.

"Of course not," she murmured assent. Tired as she was, she wanted to stay with him until she found out what was the matter.

It was a warm, pleasant evening and the french windows were open, letting onto the side veranda, so Stephen didn't bother to ring the bell. They walked along the veranda and entered directly into the breakfast room.

"He knows I'm coming. He'll probably be in the library," Stephen said absently.

"Your father?" Tildy asked, walking along beside him without much thought, simply because he hadn't told her to stop and wait.

"No, Bruce."

"Your brother? Did you fly back here to see Bruce?"

"Yes, Father said he was desperately upset and thought I should get here as quickly as possible."

Bruce was indeed in the library, dressed in his usual faded jeans and turtleneck sweater. Tildy sank down into a leather chair just inside the doorway.

Bruce whirled around when he heard them enter. His eyes were burning, his face chalky. He ignored—or didn't see—Tildy and spoke directly to Stephen.

"Well, the great statesman has returned."

"Take it easy, Bruce. Father said you were upset about the Hallett wilderness development. He asked me to come back. What is it? What's on your mind?"

For the first time Tildy noticed that the roll of plans from the developer, Walter Hallett, lay on the library table. Bruce was pointing to them, wordless for a moment in his anger.

"What about them?" Stephen asked steadily, and she marveled at how calm and controlled he seemed, how wide awake.

"You lied to me. Your whole position on conservation was a fake, wasn't it? Just to get the youth vote! Wasn't it!"

"No, it was not." Stephen picked up the plans and rolled them out flat. He started to speak but Bruce leaped across the space between them and snatched the papers. They snapped back into the roll. He flung them across the room, and the roll bounced against the wall, fell to the floor, and rolled under a couch.

"You used me. And my friends." Bruce's young face was twisted with bitterness. "I hate your guts."

Stephen's face had lost color, but his expression did not change. This was his brother talking to him like this. It made Tildy slightly sick.

155

"Bruce! Did you read the plans? Did you even look at them!"

"I don't have to. You sold us out!"

"Bruce, if I made it to the Senate I have to represent all the people. Old and young. If you will just study these plans, you'll see that they provide plenty of—Bruce, please—"

"No! I have to . . . think about things!" Bruce's voice broke. He was hurting, too. Without another word he slammed out of the room.

"He's going to cry, and he doesn't want me to see," Stephen said woodenly. He was slumping forward slightly, as if he were simply too tired to stand up straight. "I've hurt him."

"You're awfully tired," Tildy said uncertainly. "We all are." It was like a prayer. She had never been so tired in her life before. If only she could sleep. Forget. Forget about the campaign. Forget Bruce's being ashamed to cry. Forget Stephen, so tired that he bent over. Forget it all and just go to sleep. But sleep was so far away. It was across town in her own apartment. Somehow or other she had to get there and fall down on the bed and sleep. She heard herself saying to Stephen, "You really must get some rest."

Then she decided, very cautiously, that she would just lean her head against the back of the chair and rest. Just for a moment. It all seemed so vague, like some dim and sorrowful play she had watched.

The next thing she knew she was in a car, and it was stopping. Somehow—Stephen? Oh, surely not Stephen. He should be home sleeping. But it was Stephen.

"Can you wake up for a minute? I could carry you into the building but it would look odd."

"Oh, yes. Oh, I'm so sorry. Stephen, I'm so sorry. I fell asleep!" She was horrified. "Did you bring me here?"

"Yes." He was smiling that grim, tired smile. "I carried you out to the car, but I don't want to make a big thing of carrying you into your apartment building. Could you walk it?"

"Oh, yes, I'm so sorry." She scrambled out of the

car, stumbling from exhaustion. "You go back. I'm fine."

"I'll just see you to your door. You might fall asleep in the lobby."

"All right," she agreed quickly. She must not waste time by arguing.

Upstairs, in her small apartment, she said, rather clearly she thought, "The couch. It's a nice couch. I'll just lie down on the couch." The bedroom was too far away. "Won't you sit down?" she heard herself asking in dim politeness.

He remained standing at the door, and he said gently, "Don't be dumb, Tildy. If I sit down, I'll fall asleep. And if I fall asleep, I won't wake up until morning. Then I would still be here and what would the press make of that? We had a car trailing us all the way over. I have to get out of here. Can you make it to the couch?"

"Of course," she managed to say.

Go, Stephen. Get out. I want to sleep. I have to cry. She walked over to the couch. She didn't know it but she fell asleep and started to cry at the same time.

CHAPTER 16

She awoke about six o'clock, in the predawn darkness, and sat bolt upright on the couch, with the conviction that she must go somewhere and do something.

She snapped on a lamp and headed for the shower. She felt much better, much rested. Stepping out of the shower, scrubbed and wide-awake, she hurried into jeans and a T-shirt, tying up her hair with a scarf. She didn't even bother with makeup.

She hadn't driven her own car for a long time and wondered if it would start. It did. Once again she was driving through the dark morning streets of Sacramento. The street lamps were still on, but the sleeping city seemed deserted. She thought, *I'm really doing a ridiculous thing,* but went on anyhow. Soon she pulled the car to a stop before the stately entrance of the Talbot house. She didn't have a key. There was no way she could avoid ringing the bell.

She rang twice before Crandall, the butler, arrived to open the door. Crandall had not yet shaved but he was clad in his customary morning garb of white jacket over dark trousers.

"Ah—Miss Marshall?"

"Yes, Crandall." How easily she said it. "I have to see Mr. Bruce for a few minutes—something rather important. Is he here?"

"Ah—yes, Miss Marshall. He came in rather late. I daresay he's sleeping." There was, she thought, a small twinkle in Crandall's eyes.

"Which room is his? I'll just go up and wake him myself. I wouldn't have come at this awful hour, but I have to be on a plane with Mr. Stephen at eight."

"Yes, miss. Of course. These are hectic times. Mr. Bruce's room is just beyond the head of the stairs, on the left."

"Thank you." She wished for Crandall's sake that she had worn something besides jeans and T-shirt—he had never seen her when she wasn't elegantly gowned. It must have been a shock.

Quite deliberately she walked back to the Talbot library. There on the floor was the roll of plans. She picked it up and mounted the stairway. First room on the left, he had said.

She rapped on the door softly several times before there was any sound from inside. Then it was only a muffled moan. Taking this as an invitation, she opened the door and slipped silently in. She groped for a light switch and flooded the room with the light from the ceiling and two lamps.

Bruce struggled to a sitting position in the middle of an antique four-poster bed. Then she realized that beneath the covers he was naked, for he suddenly clutched the covers to his chest.

"Tildy!" he gasped, almost disbelieving that she stood before him. "What's wrong!" He stared at her glassily.

"Nothing that some common sense won't fix," she said firmly, holding the roll of plans out.

"Oh, those. If you are here to convince me that the great statesman, my brother, is one of the good guys, you can forget it."

"It will cost us our friendship," Tildy said steadily, not at all sure that her friendship meant much to Bruce. But Bruce meant a lot to Stephen, and if there was any way she could right the difference between them, she was bound to try.

Apparently her friendship was of value to Bruce because he said, rather grudgingly, "Oh, hell. All right. If it's that important to you. But for Pete's sake let me get something on."

Obediently, she walked over to the window, drew back the draperies, and stood looking down into the dark garden until he spoke again.

"Okay, let's get it over with." He stood behind her. He had sloshed water on his face; the edges of his hair were damp. He was hunched over, his fists jammed down in the pockets of a white terry cloth robe.

"I want you to look at these plans," Tildy said crisply. "Stephen says that you are very intelligent. I'd like to see if you are. Stephen also says that these plans of Hallett's show fantastically good land use and development. I believe him. I want you to study these plans." She thought she sounded somewhat like an old-time schoolteacher, but she put the roll of plans down on a table with a determined thump.

Bruce looked at her for a long time.

"You're in love with my brother, aren't you?" he asked softly.

"We are here to talk about these plans, not my emotional state," Tildy said, but she felt her face coloring.

There was just the faintest sigh from Bruce. "Forget him, Tildy." His voice was kind. "My brother is Mr. Sex Appeal himself. That and the Talbot money offer a great temptation to every woman he meets. Very early in life he learned to fend them off. You would not believe the number of chicks he has fended off—some were very nice. But he's still single at thirty-four. In fact, he's been so cautious for so long that I doubt now if he'll ever break down and actually marry anybody."

"Then he'll just have to stay single, won't he?" Tildy said levelly. She had sensed a distinct retreat or withdrawing in Bruce, and she felt a rising of slow anger against him, against Stephen. "You know, I am a little tired of this eternal Talbot hang-up about the Talbot money, this everlasting fear that all anybody wants from any Talbot is money. I'm aware that Stephen has this hang-up, too. I hope someday he realizes that money isn't

161

all he's got, that—" She stopped, half-turning. "Will you read the plans?" she demanded.

Bruce took his time answering, regarding her with a speculative look so like Stephen's.

"Yes, I will read the plans," he said finally. "I'll read them, Tildy, because you ask me to, not because I think it will change my mind. Will that satisfy you?" He added, with a half-smile, "I still like you—even if you did fall for my brother."

"That's all I ask," she answered stiffly and walked out of the room. Going down the wide stairs, she was glad that Crandall was nowhere to be seen, nor any member of the Talbot family. The great house was totally silent. Quietly, she let herself out the front door and drove back to her apartment.

She had done the best she could for Stephen. She hoped Bruce would, indeed, keep his promise to read the plans. If he did, maybe the relationship so valuable to Stephen could be salvaged and mended, and the two brothers returned to the rapport they had enjoyed before. But she was oddly despondent over it. Each was so strong in his own way, so positive, so stubborn, that a disagreement between them might be a final one—and at what emotional cost to both. A nagging ache was beginning in the back of her head.

When she was ready and waiting for Stephen, she flicked through the accumulated forwarded mail and extracted her sample ballot and voter's handbook. Uncle James had forwarded them in another envelope from San Francisco.

In the interest of saving time, she had offered to ask for an absent voter's ballot and vote by mail, and Vera had been appalled.

"Tildy, no!" she had snapped. "We won't be campaigning on Election Day, but at least we can get some news pictures of you actually going into the voting booth. All the candidates do that. It's the last fragment of publicity we get before the ax falls." So Tildy had stood embarrassed, aware that Stephen had been slightly annoyed at

162

her naive suggestion. That had been a while ago. She rarely made naive suggestions now.

They were at a hotel overlooking the sea and the twisted cypress trees of Carmel when Stephen received a call from Bruce. It was evening. She had watched Stephen throughout the day, hour by hour, doing everything carefully, not making any mistakes. The only signs that he might be under a personal strain were a too calm voice, and his avoidance of any close contact with her at all. Not once had his glance met hers throughout the day. She thought he was regretting that she had witnessed the slashing verbal attack on him by his brother, regretted her having witnessed his humiliation and hurt.

He took the call from Bruce with a look of pleased interest, the way he always accepted calls from Bruce. But he turned slightly away from the group, with seeming casualness, so that his face was averted.

The conversation was brief. They heard him say, "Yes, Bruce, what is it?" Then came a long listening silence. Then, "All right. I understand. Thanks for calling." That was all. When he replaced the receiver and turned to the group again, his eyes rested on Tildy for a moment. The expression was thoughtful.

She felt sick. Oh, surely, Bruce hadn't said anything about his discovery! So far Stephen had seemed convinced that he only held a physical attraction for her, but nothing more. He had made that very clear. She sent up a prayer that Bruce hadn't betrayed her in this fashion. She at least wanted to go out of Stephen's life with her pride intact.

When they had a moment alone together later, he said to her, "You might be interested to know that Bruce has changed his mind about Hallett's land use development." He said nothing more, and she had no way of knowing what else he knew, what other knowledge lay behind the quiet eyes and controlled face. But inwardly there was a little leaping of the heart. He had his brother back, and she, Tildy Marshall, had done that for him.

When she spoke to Uncle James that night on the

163

phone, he said, "Well, my dear, it's almost over, isn't it? The Talbots have invited me to Sacramento for the evening of Election Day. And you will be there, of course."

"Yes, I will." Stephen's sister had filled her in over the phone one evening. "I'll be with Stephen and the rest of the Talbots," she told Uncle James. "Vera, Alan, Jeremy, and the campaign people will be at the headquarters for a while, and then we'll go over to the hotel where the victory ball will be held. That's in Sacramento, Uncle James. But there are other victory balls—in five different cities, I think. Then later the Talbot party will go over to the one in Sacramento. Jean says that they've arranged for a closed circuit TV hookup, so that Stephen can talk to the other cities, all his workers and so on, you know. Will you come, Uncle James?"

"I wasn't sure. How do you feel about it? Do you want me there?"

"I want you there!" She spoke fervently.

"Then I'll be there."

As she replaced the receiver, she knew that she would need Uncle James on that evening more than she had ever needed him in her life before. Maybe some day, fifty years from now, she would be able to look back on that evening and it wouldn't hurt. But now she knew that it would take every shred of willpower, determination, and sheer guts she had to get through it, win or lose.

If Stephen lost, she faced the agony of watching him accept it, make a concession speech, and then talk to his despondent and defeated workers across the vast state of California. If he won, she might momentarily share in his triumph, relieved that he had his heart's desire, but then the full heat and glare of the publicity would turn on her about wedding plans. She could hear them now, talking over each other, thrusting the microphones into her face, jostling their cameras to get a better shot.

Somehow or other she would handle it, but for now she tried to put it out of her mind.

The last ten days of campaigning were intense. She never got more than four hours of sleep, and she was grimly proud of the fact that this was because of the extra time she spent in actual work—mingling with the public at every stop; handing out lapel buttons, leaflets, and bumper stickers; posing for pictures and giving brief interviews to any reporter who wanted one. She knew exactly what to say and do.

The night before the election Alan moaned in pretended agony about the weather report. It promised scattered showers over most of California.

"Don't people vote if it rains?" Tildy asked. There had been a general tightening and heightening of spirits all day long. It was their last day of campaigning. Tomorrow was the big day.

Jeremy cut in, "Some of the pros say that rain is good for Republicans and bad for the Democrats."

Stephen laughed. "Do the pros say anything about the Independents? And what about the Republicans and Democrats who are also undecideds?"

Then he sobered. "I'm afraid this is anybody's game, my friends. So let me take a moment now, between crises, to tell you all something. You are the ones who have worked closest to me and I've watched the job you've done. No matter how this election goes tomorrow, each of you can be certain in his or her own mind that you've done your utmost. If we lose, it will be because the people of California don't want Stephen Talbot in the Senate. If we win, you can be certain that we couldn't have done it without the excellence of your combined efforts. You have my deepest gratitude—and that's my last speech of the day. Let's all get some rest. We deserve it."

It was a gracious tribute and they were touched. For a moment Vera's eyes shimmered and both Alan and Jeremy cleared their throats, looking uncomfortable and pleased at the same time. Tildy watched Stephen covertly as he drove her to her apartment. He was at last showing strain. She wondered if he too had lost weight during the long grind. He was so muscular it was hard to tell. But for the first time there seemed a tightness about his mouth and his eyes seemed tired.

In her apartment she almost rushed to the telephone.

165

Suddenly she was shaking. Tomorrow! No. Not yet. Please! Not yet. It was too soon. They needed more time—just one more week, just a few more speeches, a few more interviews, just a little more time.

With unsteady hands she picked up the telephone receiver, almost dropping it, and began to dial. She must talk to Uncle James for a while. She must just sit down on the edge of the couch and talk to Uncle James because tomorrow was Election Day, because of Stephen, because if he lost, she couldn't bear it.

CHAPTER 17

The weather report was right. Showers came and went, and a capricious wind blew first one way, then another. She was glad she had taken the time to sew weights in the hem of her expensive and beautiful raincoat. She had chosen lavender rainwear, with a hint of gray in it, Heather, the saleswoman had said. A perky little rain hat, shaped like a fisherman's hat, was on her head. She had turned the brim up. Her face must never be hidden from the cameras. About her throat she had knotted a richly purple print scarf.

Though they were not going to campaign today, there did not seem to be enough time. They seemed surrounded by newspeople and photographers minute by minute, with Vera, Alan, and Jeremy in the background, oiling the wheels, making the arrangements.

There was a lot of excitement at Stephen's voting place in Sacramento. He kept her close beside him. Not one picture seemed to be of him alone.

There was not even a respite on the drive to San Francisco to her voting precinct. Vera had last-minute plans, details, and questions about the various victory balls to be held throughout California that night.

Tildy watched Stephen, apparently concentrating on each problem as it arose, accepting this, rejecting that, with a valid reason. Before they reached San Francisco

167

and Tildy's precinct, Jeremy and Alan had both accumulated lists of telephone calls to make.

At her precinct, Tildy posed, holding her ballot. She posed as Stephen lifted the curtain of the voting booth. She posed coming out of the curtained booth—smiling always, looking at Stephen always, to make sure that attention was directed his way. She had to do the in-and-out of the voting booth three times for the various sets of news people. And of course, there was more confusion from the TV people with their more complicated cameras, and film-taping devices.

After lunch and their return to Sacramento, a special list of key people had to be called personally. Stephen delegated a portion of it to her. Many of the names were familiar—she was getting better at remembering—people she had met, either volunteers in the campaign itself or men and women who had rallied to Stephen's support during the past months. The message to each was simple. Vera briefed her.

She hadn't minded the extra work of telephoning. That had been Stephen's idea. These were the people who had helped him and he thought they deserved a special thanks before the votes were in.

Later Stephen picked her up at her apartment, after she had dressed with great care and taken utmost pains with her makeup. She had decided to carry on the lavender theme. Her eyes, looking enormous, were faintly shadowed with lavender. Her chiffon dress, with its several layers of filmy skirt for elegant draping, was palest lavender at the top and intensified down the skirt until it was a rich lavender at the bottom. Her wrap was purple velvet, edged with a rim of white fur, with a detachable hood, which could also drape gracefully down her back.

Stephen himself looked grand in a beautifully cut suit of heavy charcoal silk, with a jacket shot with silver, over his silk shirt.

Among the assembled family and friends in the huge living room, Tildy immediately picked out Uncle James, and felt a surge of sheer joy. He was elegant! The beautiful evening clothes he had rented—probably from the same place he had got the tuxedo—must have cost him half a month's salary. The dark fabric was rich and soft, and the front of his silk shirt was formed of small, exquisite ruffles. His cuffs also had ruffles. Suddenly her tension eased. After tonight they both would drop out of sight and slowly recover from their hurts, but they were going out with banners flying.

After dinner they repaired to the game room in the vast basement, which she had never seen. Three TV sets had been set up side by side, one beamed to each major channel. It was a kind of party. Some of the men played a game of billiards with half their attention. Four others in elegant evening dress diverted themselves in a game of Ping-Pong.

After ten the first election returns started trickling in from small rural towns where the returns were easy to count. A scoreboard had been set up near the bar and Lennie Bishop, looking strange in evening clothes, kept the tally up to date.

The massive returns would come from the big city populations. And none of the returns were yet in from the vast area of southern California. In Los Angeles, with its three million people, there was an agonizing delay because of a computer breakdown in the vote-tallying section.

Mrs. Talbot found time to be with Tildy intermittently, charming, kind, pleasant as always. So was Jean, Stephen's sister, who took pains to be gracious. Maybe they realized that—win or lose—she had been a help to Stephen. Mr. Talbot spoke to her, seated in a chair near the TV sets, his cane nearby.

"Campaigns are so very strenuous," he said in his deep, gentle voice. "There is never enough time to know people. I think, my dear, in this case it is our loss." He reached over and patted her hand. She was touched. He was a person she would like to have known well.

At midnight they all got into cars and went to the great ballroom in the expensive hotel where the Sacramento Victory Ball was being held. The huge room was plastered with posters of Stephen, with a dais at one end with the lectern and microphones already set up, and a speaker system. There were two bands, an old-fashioned big dance band and a small rock group with a great deal of amplifying equipment. The place was jammed with exuberant people.

At one o'clock a cheer arose and Tildy, who had been momentarily distracted, turned to look at the scoreboard over the dais. Stephen had caught up with the Republican.

Alan, nearby, let out a happy howl. "It's the undecideds! They're deciding!" This brought a shout of laughter from those surrounding them. The big band took a break and the rock group took over, the amplifiers blasting their music so that talk was impossible. People shouted happily with nobody hearing anything but the sound of hard rock. Vera took hold of Stephen's arm and he put his head down, trying to hear her. Tildy watched him smile with a gleam of white teeth. She moved over to stand by Uncle James. He clasped her hand. Speech was impossible. Suddenly the mad music stopped.

Stephen lifted both his arms and those about them gave him their instant attention. He shouted, "The L.A. computers are fixed!" There was a wild cheer, which picked up as the word was passed through the ballroom. That meant the southern California returns would start pouring in.

Miraculously, the TV monitors, mounted high up near the ceiling, each with its own scoreboard on camera, started showing the increase. It was rapid. Stephen's count started to climb. In twenty minutes he was even with the candidate from the Democratic Party. Other cities began reporting counts. In forty-five minutes Stephen passed the Democratic candidate.

Stephen had won!

Tildy felt a surge of pure elation and gripped Uncle James's hand. Somehow during the interval of fast returns, hysterical TV anchormen, and a rising crescendo of noise in the ballroom, the Talbots had come together as a group. Shouts were rising from the hundreds of peo-

170

ple in the ballroom. Cries rose. It became the customary candidate chant.

"We want Steve. We want Steve. We want Steve."

The Talbots, with Tildy and Uncle James in their midst, made their way slowly through the mass of packed humanity that tried to make way for them. It was slow going. People reached out. Hands must be shaken, congratulations answered. It was a fantasy of delight. Total strangers were hugging each other in jubilation.

Finally, breathless, the Talbots attained the dais and grouped themselves in the background, the way a candidate's family always did. Stephen's arm went around Tildy and he pulled her close to his side as he stood at the lecturn, waiting for the din to subside.

Mr. Talbot leaned heavily on his cane, trying to hide his pride in his son, but not able to. Bruce's eyes held tears. Most of them were waving to the crowd. Tildy got a lump in her throat. Uncle James's eyes were shining and he, too, was waving to the crowd, with both arms upraised and his ruffled cuffs showing magnificently.

It was a glorious, bittersweet moment.

Soon Stephen would make a perfect victory speech, a speech of strength and humility, with his purpose and determination coming through. But for now, until the noise died down, there was nothing to do but wait.

She was very close to him, playing her part, waving and smiling along with the rest. Momentarily he pulled her to one side, away from the live microphones.

"I think you are enjoying this part of it," he said. He had to say it twice before she could hear him.

"I am." She nodded. "It's the most exciting thing in my whole life!"

He looked intently down at her for a moment and then he said, "Do you love me, Tildy?"

She heard that, but she was stunned. Bruce had told him! He knew! He would be sorry for her. He would do some kind thing and—what was Bruce's term—fend her off. He might—oh, please God, no—he might offer her some sort of extra bonus for a job well done.

"I asked if you loved me," he said, his head very

171

close to hers. From what the crowd could see they might have been talking about anything. But here was another time when only the truth would do, no matter what it cost her.

"Yes," she said steadily. "I'm sorry if that embarrasses you."

He shook his head slightly. "It's the best thing that could happen to me. Tildy, I fell in love with you a long time ago, but I thought there wasn't a chance for us, because of the work I have to do. Lately—I've been thinking, maybe I had made a mistake. But I'd hate to give it up."

The noise was terrific, but she heard almost all of what he said.

"Did you hear me?" he asked.

"Yes," she gasped.

"And you'll marry me—marry all this?"

"Oh yes." If he couldn't hear her, he could see it in her face, her eyes.

"Tildy," he said fervently, his hands gently cupping her face, caressing her hair, "there will be times of privacy, times of quiet. I promise you. I'll make life good for you—all good."

It was almost five o'clock before they were free. Mrs. Talbot invited a few people back to the Talbot house for a sunrise breakfast.

It was a beautiful, wild, wonderful time. Word had gone around through the Talbot family—how, she wasn't sure—that the engagement was real, and the marriage would take place. Everyone seemed overjoyed. Bruce grasped her hand and said fervently, "Oh, Tildy, I'm glad it's you." Uncle James couldn't stop smiling, but looked as if he wanted to cry, too.

It was clear, bright daylight before she got a moment alone with Stephen. He showed her to a guest room. A servant had been dispatched to get some of her things from her apartment. Mrs. Talbot had insisted that she stay on with them for a few hours' sleep. At her doorway, Stephen stopped, his hands on her slim shoulders.

"Are you still sure? You weren't just carried away by that crowd yelling, 'We want Steve'—whoever he is."

"No, Stephen," she laughed.

Then he kissed her. Her alone. No cameras. No one to see. No one near. Her bones felt as if they would melt. Her arms went around his neck.

"Well," he whispered softly. "I guess that leaves no doubt."

He looked down at her searchingly for a moment. "Tildy, I have to tell you something else. As I promised, I intend to be the best Senator California ever sent to Washington, if it's my power. But only for two terms."

"I—don't understand. What will you do then? Go into your father's law firm, where you worked before?"

"No." His voice was rock-hard again. "At the end of my second Senate term there will be an election for Governor in California. I intend to be the best Governor this state ever had. For two terms." His eyes were smiling now. "Could you handle being the Governor's Lady for eight years?"

"Yes!" she said quickly. This time her voice was quite shaky, but she didn't care. "I can handle that!" Her eyes were shining.

He reached up and touched her cheek ever so softly. "Don't you want to know what comes after that?"

"You mean—that isn't all?" She was beginning to feel slightly stunned, but knowing him as well as she knew him now, she could not doubt it. Whatever it was he thought he had to do, he would do it.

Sudden stark fright skipped across the surface of her mind, but at the same time she knew it didn't matter. Whatever it was, she needed to go along. They were in it together. Then—oh, no! Not that! He couldn't mean that! She looked directly up into his eyes. He did mean that. He was smiling when he said it.

"Tildy, after my second term as California Governor, how would you like to go back to Washington? Live in the White House? How would you like to be First Lady?"

Love—the way you want it!

Candlelight Romances